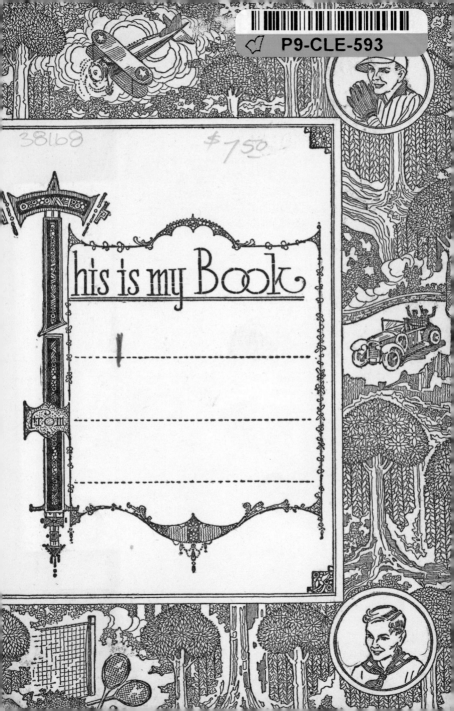

This is my Book

"AND", SAID BUDDY, "IF YOU DON'T PROCESS YOUR TIN
CANS I'LL TACK THIS NOTICE TO YOUR HOUSE."

"Buddy's Victory Club"

(See page 131)

Buddy's Victory Club

or

A Boy and a Salvage Campaign

BY

HOWARD R. GARIS

*Author of Buddy and The Indian Chief, Buddy in
Dragon Swamp, Teddy and The Mystery Dog,
The Curlytops, Uncle Wiggily, Etc.*

ILLUSTRATED

NEW YORK
CUPPLES & LEON COMPANY

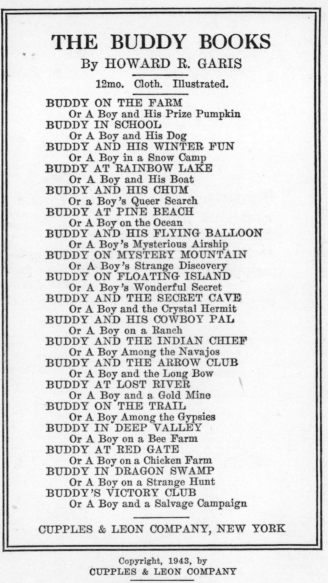

THE BUDDY BOOKS

By HOWARD R. GARIS

12mo. Cloth. Illustrated.

BUDDY ON THE FARM
Or A Boy and His Prize Pumpkin
BUDDY IN SCHOOL
Or A Boy and His Dog
BUDDY AND HIS WINTER FUN
Or A Boy in a Snow Camp
BUDDY AT RAINBOW LAKE
Or A Boy and His Boat
BUDDY AND HIS CHUM
Or a Boy's Queer Search
BUDDY AT PINE BEACH
Or A Boy on the Ocean
BUDDY AND HIS FLYING BALLOON
Or A Boy's Mysterious Airship
BUDDY ON MYSTERY MOUNTAIN
Or A Boy's Strange Discovery
BUDDY ON FLOATING ISLAND
Or A Boy's Wonderful Secret
BUDDY AND THE SECRET CAVE
Or A Boy and the Crystal Hermit
BUDDY AND HIS COWBOY PAL
Or A Boy on a Ranch
BUDDY AND THE INDIAN CHIEF
Or A Boy Among the Navajos
BUDDY AND THE ARROW CLUB
Or A Boy and the Long Bow
BUDDY AT LOST RIVER
Or A Boy and a Gold Mine
BUDDY ON THE TRAIL
Or A Boy Among the Gypsies
BUDDY IN DEEP VALLEY
Or A Boy on a Bee Farm
BUDDY AT RED GATE
Or A Boy on a Chicken Farm
BUDDY IN DRAGON SWAMP
Or A Boy on a Strange Hunt
BUDDY'S VICTORY CLUB
Or A Boy and a Salvage Campaign

CUPPLES & LEON COMPANY, NEW YORK

DEDICATED

To the boys and girls of the United
States of America who, by their
hard and unselfish work in collecting scrap, including tin cans,
helped the United Nations to
Victory.

HOWARD R. GARIS

CONTENTS

CHAPTER I

ALARM AT NIGHT

THERE was much excitement in Mount-chester where Buddy Martyne lived. Not that Buddy, or his two special chums, Tom Gordon and Harry Clee, were much excited at the moment. But a great many grown persons were.

Mayor Doremus had issued a proclamation calling upon all citizens to join in a big scrap drive for victory.

"All sorts of scrap is needed to help win the war," declared Mayor Doremus, speaking to a meeting of citizens at City Hall. "We want old iron, old lead, old brass, rubber and tin cans. Especially tin cans. Now, ladies and gentlemen, the scrap drive is on. Let's see it through to victory!"

1

There was considerable applause and then much talk. The men and women, hastily formed into a number of scrap collecting committees, began to make plans.

"Can't we get the boys and girls of Mountchester to help in this drive?" asked Mrs. Clayton Martyne. She was Buddy's mother.

"We certainly can and we will," said the mayor. "It's a good idea. I'll telephone to the school. I'll ask the principal, Mr. Pardin, to enlist the pupils in our scrap drive. We must not only reach our quota, as set by Governor Mendalin, but we must exceed it. I'll telephone now. Meanwhile, ladies and gentlemen, complete your committees and get busy."

The mayor hastened to the telephone. Mrs. Martyne began to talk to a group of men and women neighbors who had been sitting near her.

"I should think your son, Buddy, would fit right into this project," said Mrs. Tooker.

"I have no doubt he will when he hears about it," said Mrs. Martyne.

"I never saw a boy with such energy," declared Mrs. Watson. "I guess it must come from his lovely auburn hair," she added with a laugh.

"Don't let Buddy hear you call his hair anything but red," said Mrs. Martyne. "He's proud of it. And I think it must help him to do some of the things he does."

"It surely must," said Mrs. Tooker. "Otherwise I don't see how he ever helped catch those dreadful dragon lizards down in Florida last Summer."

"Yes, that was quite an adventure," admitted Buddy's mother. "But now, ladies, we must make plans for having a systematic drive after all the scrap in our little city. Every last ounce will be needed to help us win the war."

Thereupon Mrs. Martyne and all the other grown-up citizens, men and women of Mountchester, began talking ways and means of getting out the scrap iron, lead, rubber and tin for reclamation in the war effort.

By this time Mayor Doremus had finished

speaking to Principal Pardin. And the principal, who had been called away from his last little talk to the pupils on this last day of school, came back to the platform.

"I am sure, boys and girls," he said, "that you all expect to have good times this vacation—this long, Summer vacation."

"He said something that time," muttered Ike Blatter. He was one of the older boys of the school and, with Sid Monson, Jake Turner and a few others, made up a group that often got into trouble.

"I'm not going to open a book until next September," declared Sid Monson. "Vacation is right—I'm going to do nothing but loaf."

"And maybe fish," added Jake.

These three were talking rather loudly and Mr. Pardin glanced in their direction. The three cronies were seated near Buddy, Tom and Harry and, for a moment, it seemed to Mr. Pardin that it was Buddy, or one of his chums, who had interrupted. The principal said:

"Richard, I wish you wouldn't talk when I am talking, even if it is the last day and discipline is somewhat relaxed. I have an important announcement to make." The principal must have been quite provoked to call Buddy "Richard," which, of course was his name. But everyone always called him Buddy.

"If you please, Mr. Pardin, I didn't say anything," spoke the red-haired lad in honest denial.

Then Ike, perhaps because he realized several sitting near him knew he was the culprit, raised his hand and said:

"It was me, Mr. Pardin."

Not pausing to correct Ike's faulty grammar, the principal smiled and said:

"Well, because you have been honest, I shall excuse you. But please keep quiet just a few moments longer. Then you may talk as much as you please, for classes will be dismissed."

Mr. Pardin gave the mayor's message and said he was quite sure the pupils of his

school would do all they could to get in the
scrap.

"And by 'scrap' I mean odds and ends,
which are now so vitally needed to help us
win the war," said the principal. "That's
the sort of 'scrap' I mean, not what some of
you boys say when you have a fight. Though
of course we must fight for victory," con-
cluded the principal.

School was then dismissed for the long
Summer vacation. The boys and girls were
excited now by the prospect of many happy
weeks in which they might have fun. They
were also thrilled by the prospect of doing
their share in collecting scrap.

"And speaking of scrap," said Buddy to
his chums as they hurried out of school, "I
would have gotten into a real scrap with Ike
Blatter if he hadn't owned up he was doing
the talking."

"I should say so!" agreed Tom.

"And I'd have helped you if it came to a
fight," added Harry.

"But that's all over now," went on Buddy.

"What we have to do is to help collect this iron, brass, rubber and tin-can scrap for the war victory. You fellows going to come in with me," asked Buddy of his two chums, "or do you want to go on your own?" He ran his fingers through his red hair as he paused on the edge of the school playground.

"We'll come in with you," said Tom.

"Of course," said Harry.

"Then we'll form a sort of company," went on Buddy who was a natural leader among the boys. "We three, and maybe some others, if they want to join, will get all the scrap we can and turn it in as our share into the general collection the mayor's getting up."

"We'll have a sort of scrap club," suggested Tom.

"Why not call it Buddy's club, as long as he thought of it?" asked Harry. "If we had some sort of a shack we could put the scrap there and hold meetings like in a regular club. Say, that's an idea—Buddy's Club! How about it?"

"Nothing doing!" snapped the red-haired lad. "The club idea is all right, but it isn't going to be called 'Buddy's Club.' If we call it anything we'll name it the 'Victory Club.' That's what it is going to be."

"Well, all right, Victory Club, then," agreed Harry.

"As for a place to meet, we can have half our garage," went on Buddy. "My father has given up one of our cars. Said we didn't need two cars, with the war on and tires and gas being rationed. So one half our garage is empty."

"That'll make a swell club house!" exclaimed Tom.

"Swell!" agreed Harry.

"Then let's go there now and sort of look it over," suggested Buddy.

"Can we pile the scrap we get in there?" asked Tom.

"Sure," Buddy agreed.

"Say! This is going to be great—Buddy's Victory Club!" exclaimed Harry.

"Cut out the Buddy part," advised the red-haired owner of the name.

But in spite of Buddy's objection the name stuck and from then, until long afterward, the club was associated with his name.

To see the three chums hurrying toward the Martyne garage would have given the impression none of them had seen it before. There had been no change in the building, but now new ideas were connected with it. The boys felt they had a personal share in it.

"What are you going to do this Summer, Buddy?" asked Tom as the trio neared the Martyne home on a maple-shaded street in the residential section of Mountchester.

"Stay home," said the red-haired lad.

"Stay home!" echoed Harry. "Why, you always go away and have adventures and all like that."

"Not this Summer," said Buddy. "Dad and Mother decided that now we are at war, it's no time to go off pleasuring. Besides, gas is scarce, and dad said the tires on the one car he's keeping aren't any too hot. He's only going to drive when there's no other way."

"Then you won't be doing any dragon

lizard hunting this Summer," said Tom.

"Not a dragon or a liz," laughed Buddy. "I'm going to get in the scrap."

"We'll help!" chorused Tom and Harry.

"That's what the Victory Club is for," added Buddy. "Well, here's the club house, fellows," he went on as they reached the garage.

"Say, this'll be swell!" declared Tom. "It's just made for a club."

The garage was divided in two parts by a wooden partition. One section was now vacant, Mrs. Martyne having turned in her car for the duration.

"After it's cleaned up a little it won't be so bad," admitted Buddy. "But let's go in the house now. I'm hungry. I know Lola baked some molasses cookies this morning. If I hand her the right line of talk she'll give us some. And maybe some milk."

"Oh, boy!" murmured Tom and Harry.

Lola Wagg, the Martyne maid, was not hard to convince, after Buddy told how hungry he and his chums were.

"Oh, you're always hungry!" laughed the maid. "Wait until I throw this tin can on the ash pile—"

"Wait! Hold on! Stop!" commanded Buddy, taking the can from Lola. "Don't you know that's valuable?"

"Don't be silly, Buddy!" laughed Lola. "It's only an old tin can—well, not very old, for I just opened it and took out some peaches for supper. But—"

"It is valuable," insisted the red-haired lad. "It's part of the scrap our club is going to collect to help us to victory. But the can will have to be processed first."

"Processed? What's the joke?" asked Tom.

"It isn't a joke. Tell you later," said Buddy. "Now let's eat."

This the boys did, meanwhile making plans for collecting all the scrap they could. They separated when it was nearly supper time and Mrs. Martyne came home from the City Hall meeting.

Tom and Harry agreed to come over early

in the morning and help Buddy clean the unused half of the garage for a club house.

At supper that night Buddy asked his father for permission to do this.

"Of course," agreed Mr. Martyne. "I'm glad, Buddy, that you and your chums are going to help with the scrap drive. Use the garage as much as you please."

"Thank you, Dad," said Buddy. Then, while his father and mother, after supper, talked over their plans for forming committees to solicit various kinds of scrap from the citizens of Mountchester, Buddy went out in the early moonlight to look over the garage.

He had seen it hundreds of times before, but now it took on a new and added interest in his eyes.

"It will be a dandy little clubhouse—a 'Victory' Clubhouse," he said as he turned back toward the house.

As he did so he thought he saw a moving, slinking shadow, cast by the bright moon, around one corner of the garage.

"I wonder who that can be?" thought the red-haired lad. "I guess it was a stray dog. Well, tomorrow Tom, Harry and I will start collecting scrap. I must teach Lola how to process tin cans, too. The government needs all the tin it can get, now the Japs have cut off our regular supply."

Buddy went to bed rather early that night. He planned to arise early, also, and get his plans under way. For several hours he slept soundly. Then, suddenly, he was awakened by a loud noise. It came from the direction of the garage and Buddy's bedroom window gave him a good view of the building.

"Sounded like one of the garage windows being slammed down," thought Buddy as he raised from his pillow and listened intently.

"Bang!" There it was again.

"That was a window all right!" exclaimed Buddy. "Some one's trying to get in our garage!"

He leaped out of bed.

CHAPTER II

SASH WEIGHTS

BUDDY wasn't certain of what he ought to do. He stood at his open bedroom window, in his pajamas. The moonlight was streaming in. It cast a silvery glow over the back yard, the garden to one side and on the other side the garage—Buddy's Victory Club. At least half of the building came under that head.

The red-haired boy peered out. It was very still and quiet. If any dogs had been barking at the moon they had now ceased and were sound asleep. Buddy wished he had a dog.

"If I had I'd call him now, and then I'd go out and see what made our garage windows slam down," murmured Buddy. "I wish I had old Bungo now."

But wishing was in vain. Old Bungo had gone where all good dogs go.

14

"I'm going to get a dog," decided Buddy. "He can come along with Tom, Harry and me when we are scouting around for scrap."

Then the red-haired lad gave over thinking about the possibility of a dog for the more immediate topic of the alarm in the night. He leaned out of the window to get a better look, pushing up the screen. He could see nothing. No more noises came from the garage.

"But I sure heard a window bang," decided Buddy. "Maybe it's thieves. They forced up a window to get in and it slammed down when they got out. But they couldn't take dad's car through a window. And the doors aren't open." He could see the four big doors of the garage all closed. The moonlight glinted on their painted surfaces.

"I wonder—" began Buddy, half talking to himself.

And then, as he drew in his head, there was a sudden, loud slam in his own room. The wire screen he had been supporting on his shoulders while he leaned out of the window, had slid down with a resounding crash as he pulled in his head.

"Oh, gosh!" murmured Buddy. "That'll be sure to wake mother—and dad," he added as he heard a noise in the room, down the hall, where his parents slept.

A moment later his father's voice called:

"Buddy, is that you?"

"Yes, Dad."

"What was that noise?"

"My screen fell down," said the red-haired boy.

"Do you mean it tumbled out?" asked his mother. "If it did close the window, or the house will be full of mosquitoes."

"No'm, it just slid down. I had it up," said Buddy.

"Why were you raising your screen in the middle of the night, Buddy?" asked Mr. Martyne. Buddy could hear his father snap on a light and open his bedroom door.

"I heard a noise out in the garage," Buddy answered. "I raised the screen so I could look out and listen better. And when I pulled my head in it fell down—I mean the screen fell down."

Buddy could hear his father chuckle.

"I think there are thieves in our garage— or maybe they tried to get in and a window slammed down and they got scared and ran away," Buddy explained.

"Nonsense!" said Mr. Martyne as he entered Buddy's room.

"I certainly heard one of the garage windows slam down," Buddy insisted. "That's what woke me up."

"Well, they couldn't take my car through a window," said Mr. Martyne as he peered out. "And if they got in through a window, and opened the doors to drive out the car, they couldn't get very far. I have barely enough gas to get to the filling station and turn in a coupon to have my tank partly filled. I guess you dreamed it, Buddy."

"No, Dad, I didn't dream," insisted the red-haired lad. "I sure heard a noise. It was a window slamming down. You know the garage windows go up and down easy.

They could get your tires off and out through a window, couldn't they, Dad?"

"Whew! I didn't think of tires!" admitted Mr. Martyne. "They are almost as valuable now as a car. I'll go out and take a look."

"May I come?" asked Buddy, putting his bare feet into slippers and reaching for his bath robe.

"No, you stay here," ordered Mr. Martyne.

"But, Dad," objected Buddy, "if I could help Captain Bill Haydon catch those dragon lizards—" Buddy paused and waited.

Mr. Martyne scratched his tousled head in bewilderment. Then with a little smile he said:

"Yes, I guess you are growing up, Buddy. I sort of forget you aren't in the kindergarten. Come along!"

Buddy was ready in a moment and had his flashlight.

"What is it, Clayton?" called Mrs. Martyne.

"I heard a noise in the garage," Buddy explained. "A window slammed down. Somebody is after dad's tires."

"We don't know that," his father reminded the red-haired boy.

"I'm sure it is!" Buddy insisted. "I'll help you catch 'em!"

"Buddy, you're not going out there!" exclaimed Mrs. Martyne.

"Aw, Mother! Didn't I go after the dragon lizards?"

Then, as had her husband, Mrs. Martyne suddenly realized that Buddy was no longer a child. She gave her consent by saying:

"Well, be careful."

"I will," promised Buddy, happy that he was to be allowed to accompany his father on the investigation of the night alarm.

"It seems quiet enough out at the garage now," said Mr. Martyne, as he and Buddy stepped away from Buddy's window which gave a moonlighted view of the scene.

"They either got away with the tires, or they were scared away by the window that slammed down," was Buddy's opinion.

He and his father cautiously opened the back kitchen door and stepped into the yard. The moon was full and very bright.

Suddenly, as father and son neared the garage, they heard a noise from inside. It was the sound of running feet and, a moment later the distinct sound of a falling window was heard.

"What did I tell you?" whispered Buddy.

"I guess you were right, son," said Mr. Martyne. "You stay back, Buddy. "I don't want you to run into danger."

"Aw, dad—"

Buddy was protesting but he obeyed, and then he saw something which caused him to exclaim:

"There they go, Dad! Two of 'em—running away from in back. They got out the back window. Look!"

The rear of the garage was in the shadow.
And back of the garage were a number of
trees, so that any thieves emerging in that
direction could not plainly be seen. But
Mr. Martyne and Buddy saw two shadowy
figures running away in the darkened area
back of the garage. The figures scudded
beneath the trees, still in the shadow, and
seemed to be laden with heavy objects.

"They got your tires, Dad!" called Buddy,
no longer whispering.

"No, I don't think so," said Mr. Martyne.
"They're carrying something they took
from my garage, but not tires. I could see
tires if they were carrying them. It isn't
tires."

"Then what is it?" asked Buddy.

"I don't know. But we'll find out!" declared Mr. Martyne in firm tones. "Hey,
you!" he called after the two retreating,
shadowy forms. "Stop where you are!
Bring back what you took!"

But the figures did not stop. Nor did they

return. They ran on and on until their
shadows merged into the shadows of a patch
of woods back of the Martyne home.

"They got away," said Buddy regretfully.

"Maybe it's just as well," said Mr. Martyne. "But they didn't take my car nor my
tires."

"They got something—what was it?"
asked Buddy.

"We'll find out," his father said.

A key to the big locked doors of the garage hung in a secret place beneath a side
window of the building. Mr. Martyne kept
it there so that if he forgot his own bunch
of keys, he could get in. With this secret
key he opened one of the doors.

"Let me have your flashlight, Buddy," he
said.

Buddy switched it on and gave it to his
father. Swinging the circle of light around
that half of the garage where his car stood,
Mr. Martyne soon proved that the auto had
not been disturbed, nor had any of the tires
been taken.

Then Mr. Martyne focused the light on a side window. He uttered an exclamation of surprise.

"The sash weights!" he said. "They're gone! They cut the cords and took away the weights. That's why the window slammed down."

"But what would any thieves want with cast iron window sash weights, Dad?" asked Buddy.

"I think it's because Mountchester has started a victory scrap campaign, Buddy," said his father. "All junk is valuable now—especially iron. Scrap thieves have been here. I think they must have carried away all my garage window sash weights. They're gone from this window. We'll take a look at the others."

Wonderingly Buddy followed his father into the other part of the garage—the room that was to be the meeting place for Buddy's Victory Club.

CHAPTER III

FLASHING Buddy's light on the window in the club side of the garage, Mr. Martyne disclosed that the same thing had happened.

"They got these sash weights, too," he said.

The light gleamed on two oblong openings, or pockets, one on each side of the window. These pockets had contained cylindrical, iron weights, two in each pocket, which counter-balanced the weights of the two window sashes. The weights made it easier to raise and lower the sashes.

Both side pockets were empty, but in each one could be seen the ends of the cords that had held the weights. One end of a cord had been fast to a weight, the other end was still fast to the sash.

"Yes, they took the weights from here,

too," said Mr. Martyne. "And the back window," he added as the light revealed empty weight pockets there. "They made a clean job of it. That's what the men we saw running away were carrying, Buddy," said his father. "Sash weights from my garage."

"How did they know the weights were here?" asked the red-haired lad. "Oh, of course," he said quickly, as he saw his father smiling. "All garage windows have sash weights."

"Most of them, I suppose," admitted Mr. Martyne. "But all sash weights aren't as easy to steal as ours were."

"Why?" asked Buddy. This time his father explained.

"Some garages," Mr. Martyne said, "have inside walls that are covered with small, narrow boards, called ceiling boards. These are nailed over the uprights, or two-by-fours, as they are called. These ceiling boards make the garage warmer. Most garages that are heated have inside boards. And the inside boards go over the window weight pockets so the weights are hidden from sight.

"But our garage, not having inside boards, has the sash weights exposed. I mean our garage *had* exposed sash weights," and Mr. Martyne emphasized the word had. "They are gone now—the weights. Not that it will do us any harm. I'll just have to put nails under each upper sash to keep them from dropping. And when I raise a lower sash I'll have to prop it up with a stick."

"I suppose," said Buddy, "that when the burglars took the weights from the upper sashes, they fell down with a bang and that's what woke me up."

"You suppose correctly, Buddy," admitted his father. "But all the upper sashes didn't fall. This one," and he motioned to the side window of the little club house, "was too tight to fall. But the others did."

"And you think the thieves took our sash weights for the scrap collection?" asked Buddy.

"Yes," said his father.

"Why didn't they come around and collect them just as Tom and Harry and I are going to collect scrap?" asked Buddy. "You'd have given them the weights, wouldn't you?"

"Yes," said Mr. Martyne, "I would. Just as I would have probably turned them over to you and your chums. But I don't believe the thieves who took my weights will turn them in to the Mountchester scrap collection."

"Why not?" asked Buddy. "That would be cheating, wouldn't it?"

"Yes, but I don't believe these chaps would stop at cheating," spoke Mr. Martyne. "They know scrap iron brings good prices from junk dealers now. So they probably plan to get a lot of sash weights, and other scrap iron, sell it for junk and keep the money."

"All the Mountchester scrap is going to be sold to junk men," said Buddy. "Our principal said so."

"Yes," admitted Mr. Martyne, "but that

will be different. The money the junk men pay for the city's scrap will be turned over to Red Cross or the U.S.O."

"The United Service Organizations—I know about them," said Buddy. "So these thieves are going to keep the scrap money for themselves, instead of having it used to help bring victory?" said the red-haired boy angrily. "They shouldn't do that. They ought to be found out and—and punished—maybe be sent to jail!"

"Something ought to be done to them," admitted Mr. Martyne. "But I don't believe they will be caught."

Buddy had his own opinion about this but he did not tell it.

"We might as well go back to bed," suggested Mr. Martyne. "We can't do any good staying out here. The mischief has been done. After all, losing my sash weights isn't much. I would have turned them in any how. A lot of us volunteered to do this at a meeting in the mayor's office this afternoon. The mayor suggested that very few garage windows were ever opened anyhow, so the weights wouldn't be missed.

"I don't know how many garages there are in Mountchester, with open sash-weight pockets," went on Buddy's father. "But, on the whole, I would say they ought to contribute considerable to the scrap pile—if they aren't stolen."

"How much does each weight weigh?" asked Buddy.

"About four pounds," his father answered.

Buddy did some fast mental arithmetic. There were six windows in his club house garage, two on each side and two in the rear. Each window had four weights.

"That's twenty-four weights at four pounds each," murmured Buddy. "Four times twenty-four—why that's ninety-six pounds of scrap iron!" he exclaimed. "No wonder those thieves sort of staggered as they ran away. Each one was carrying about fifty pounds."

"Perhaps a bit more," said Mr. Martyne.

"The weights might have scaled over four pounds each. Well, they're gone and we'd better get back to bed." Like Buddy, Mr. Martyne was wearing slippers and a bath robe. "Your mother is getting anxious," went on Buddy's father. "She's looking out of her window."

Buddy saw his mother's head framed in her illuminated bedroom window.

"It's all right," he called to her. "I mean dad and I are all right. But it's all wrong with the scrap collection."

"Wrong with the scrap collection?" exclaimed Mrs. Martyne. "Why, Buddy, what do you mean? Is the war over?"

"No, it's just started for those fellows who stole our sash weights!" declared the red-haired lad. "I'm going to have 'em arrested. Why, those sash weights would have gone into our club scrap. Just wait until I catch those sash weight thieves."

Buddy didn't intend any joke but his father laughed. Then Buddy started to jump up in the air and clap his heels to-

gether three times, a trick his uncle had
taught him. But you can't click your heels
when you are wearing slippers, as Buddy
soon discovered.

"Wait until I tell our club what happened," he said as he and his father went in
the house to explain to Mrs. Martyne.

Buddy didn't go to sleep again very
quickly. His mind was filled with many
thoughts, in which the new Victory Club
played a part.

After breakfast next morning, Lola Wagg
gave Buddy a tin can from which she had
just taken some apple sauce.

"Here's a can for you to address," she
said. "Though I don't see that there's much
room for writing," and she indicated the
printed and pictured label.

"Oh, it's *process*—not *address!*" laughed
Buddy. "I'll tell you about that later.
We've got to process all our tin cans before
we can turn them in for scrap."

"Tin cans are tin cans, addressed or processed or what not," said Lola. Buddy did

not stop to argue. He hurried to get Tom
and Harry, bringing them back to the new
club.

"We've got to clean this place up," said
Buddy. "We've got to get in a table and
some chairs. And some more members.
Three aren't enough."

"I know a lot of fellows who will want to
join," said Tom.

"So do I," spoke Harry.

"There's time enough for that," said
Buddy. "But I agree that we do need more
members. There's a lot of scrap in Mountchester that we fellows have got to search
out and turn in. Did you hear what happened last night?"

"Where?" asked Tom.

"Here," said Buddy. "In our garage.
Look at the windows."

Tom and Harry looked but did not quite
understand.

"It's the sash weights," explained the red-
haired boy. "They were stolen last night.
Maybe other garages were robbed."

He stood in front of his two chums, ruffling his red hair. Tom tossed his black hair out of his eyes and Harry ran a finger or two through his brown curls. He hated those curls, but the girls thought they were "cute."

"The meeting will please come to order," spoke Buddy in the tones he used when he sometimes presided at Boy Scout sessions. "And the first business is detective work," he added.

"Detective work?" exclaimed Tom.

"Yes," said Buddy.

"I thought this was a Victory Club," said Harry.

"It is," declared Buddy. "But first we've got to do some detective work. Listen!"

CHAPTER IV

RED CLUES

BUDDY'S chums listened. They generally did when the red-haired lad had anything to say. And, generally, Buddy knew what he was talking about. He hadn't planned to help capture those dragon lizards without knowing what he was doing.

Buddy had taken part in many adventures. From the first, as told in the initial book of this series "Buddy on The Farm," to the volume just before this, "Buddy in Dragon Swamp," our small hero was always active and on the alert.

He was no less so this time, and he was filled with enthusiasm about doing what he could to help win the victory.

"It's this way," said Buddy when Tom and Harry had given him their complete attention. "You can see where thieves got in our garage last night and took our sash

weights. That wouldn't be much of a rob-
bery except at just this time when every bit
of scrap iron counts to help win the war."

"Hurray!" shouted Tom.

"Three cheers for our side!" added
Harry.

"Cut out the cheering until we get something to cheer about," Buddy advised. He
noted that Tom and Harry were shifting
uneasily about, first on one foot and then on
the other.

"I know you're tired standing around,"
said Buddy. "But we'll get some chairs and
a table in here as soon as I show you fellows
the red clues."

"Red clues!" exclaimed his chums.

"Sure. Look here!" exclaimed Buddy.
"If you're going to do detective work, as we
are, you got to look for clues. Here are
some." He pointed to several red splashes
on the frames of the side window in the club
house section of the garage.

"Blood!" cried Tom.

"The sash-weight thieves must have cut

themselves when they broke in last night,"
added Harry.

"No," said Buddy, shaking his red head.
"In the first place the thieves didn't break
in. They just raised a rear window. We
never lock the garage windows—at least we
haven't up to now—for I guess dad figured
nobody could take a car out of the window.
And they couldn't get the car past our house
along the drive without waking me up."

"You heard the thieves last night, you
say?" asked Tom.

"Sure," said Buddy. "When they cut
the sash weight ropes, and one of the windows slid down, it would wake up anybody."

"All right, Detective Martyne," said
Harry. "The thieves didn't break in but
they got in."

"And when the window fell down," said
Tom, "the glass broke and the thieves cut
themselves and splashed blood on the window frames. How's that for detective
work."

"Punk!" said Buddy with a laugh which took the sting out of the word. "But I'll give you another chance. Take a look at those red splashes on the window frame."

Tom and Harry scanned the marks closely.

"We ought to have a magnifying glass to do real detective work," Tom said.

"Run your finger over the marks," suggested Buddy. His two chums did so and Harry exclaimed:

"They feel like red paint."

"They are red paint," said Buddy. "But they are clues just the same."

"You mean the thieves brought red paint in your garage and daubed up the window?" asked Tom.

"They must have had a lot of time," commented Harry.

"They didn't," said Buddy. "I was awake too quick. But is that paint fresh, I ask you?"

Tom and Harry looked at their fingers.

They were not smeared with the red marks as would have happened if the paint had been fresh.

"It's old paint," said Tom.

"I know it," said Buddy. "I ought to know for I put it there myself some time ago."

"You mean to make detective clues?" asked Harry.

"No, it was an accident," said the red-haired boy. "I was making a box and I wanted to paint it. I brought it out here and put it on a bench near the window where there was a good light.

"I tried my brush on the window frame to see if I had the right color of paint and that's how the marks got there. Now you understand, don't you?"

"No," said Tom, "I don't."

"And I don't, either," added his chum Harry, shaking his head of curly brown hair. "I can't see why red paint marks on the window frame of your garage, Buddy, has

anything to do with the thieves who took
the sash weights.''

"Don't you?'' asked Buddy with a smile.
"Would it mean anything if I told you that
when I tried my brush on the window frames
I got some paint on the iron sash weights?
In fact I daubed some on when I wanted to
clean my brush. The iron weights are rough
and are swell for cleaning paint brushes.''

Suddenly looks of intelligence and under-
standing broke over the faces of Tom and
Harry. They laughed and Harry said:

"You mean the red paint marks are still
on the sash weights?''

"On some of them,'' Buddy said. "And
the thieves will probably sell all the sash
weights from our garage, and maybe from
other garages, to some junk man in one par-
cel. They'll want to get rid of them quick
before they are caught.''

"I get it now!'' exclaimed Tom.

"So do I,'' said Harry. "We've only got
to look for a junkman who has bought sash

weights, some with red paint on, and we'll
have the scrap thieves."

"Yes," agreed Buddy, "but it won't be as
easy as all that. But that's what I meant by
detective work. And, now that you have
the idea of what we've got to do, let's get
some tables and chairs and other things and
fix this club house up a little. We're going
to have a lot of meetings here."

"Are we going to take in more members?"
asked Tom.

"Sure," said Buddy. "We need lots of
fellows in order to make our drive successful."

"Three's hardly enough," spoke Harry.
"Who'll we get?"

"Oh, there will be plenty," said Buddy.
"Now let's get this place fixed up so we can
sit down and do some real work in this victory scrap campaign. Then we'll hunt
around for the sash-weight thieves."

From Buddy's house a table and some
chairs were taken. They were up in the
attic and Mrs. Martyne gladly gave permission for their use. From the homes of Harry

and Tom other furnishings for the little club house were obtained.

"Say, it begins to look like a real club now," said Tom as he and his chums stood outside and looked in for an observation.

Just then three girls came strolling into the Martyne yard. One was Agnes Randall, Buddy's cousin and the others were Lucy, sister to Tom, and Mary, sister to Harry.

"Oh, what a nice club house," said Agnes.

"It's cute," declared Lucy Gordon.

"Are you going to have any more members than just you three boys?" asked Mary Clee.

"Sure," said Buddy.

"Any girls?" asked Agnes Randall.

"No!" exclaimed the three boys in a chorus.

For a moment none of the girls said anything. Then Lucy slowly remarked:

"Come on. I guess they won't want the nice window curtains we made for the club house. Well, we can join some other club. Come on!"

CHAPTER V

TREASURE TROVE

FOR a moment Buddy and his chums watched the three girls turn as if they were going to walk down the drive. Then Tom said, as if talking to himself:

"Curtains on the windows—they would look nice."

"And lots of clubs have girl members," added Harry. "They could run errands and sweep the place out."

"Look here!" exclaimed Buddy. "I don't mind the girls coming in if you fellows don't. And they could fix up the club house nice. We won't have time if we're going to collect scrap. What say?"

"I say let 'em in," was Tom's vote.

"It's all right with me," added Harry.

"I don't mind," commented Buddy. Then he called: "Hey, girls. We just had a meeting and decided to let you join the Victory Club."

"It doesn't take you long to hold a meeting," laughed Agnes.

"Not when such nice girls as you three ask to join," said Buddy.

"Oh, thank you!" chorused the three. And Agnes added:

"But we really thank you, and we want to join and help. If it's going to be a real club, with other girls and boys in it to help get in the scrap, the club house ought to look nice. It will help to attract prospective members."

"And curtains are only a start," said Mary Clee. "I thought of them when you boys were over at our house getting a table and chair."

"I can get a nice rug," added Lucy. "It's old and has a few holes in it, but it will be better than the bare concrete floor."

"A lot better," agreed Buddy. "I didn't think about dolling up the club house, but it's a good idea. We can work and make plans just as well in a nice looking place as we can in a shack."

"Better, I would say," commented Mary.

"Well, thanks a lot," spoke Buddy.

"Can we start now putting up the curtains?" asked Agnes.

"Sure," Buddy gave permission. "And bring in anything else you think would look good. We'll need more chairs if we're going to take a lot of fellows and girls into the club."

"I can get chairs," said Agnes.

"And I know there's an old electric lamp up in our attic," said Lucy. "It's a little dented but it gives good light."

"That's so!" exclaimed Buddy. "We'll have to meet nights pretty often, I guess. And we'll need a better light than that one." He indicated a single unshaded electric bulb dangling from the ceiling.

"Say, this sure will be like a real club!" said Tom.

"With lights and a carpet on the floor," added Harry.

"Well, come on, fellows," Buddy called to his chums. "We'll leave the girls to doll-up the club."

"Where are you going?" asked Lucy.

"After thieves," Buddy informed her.

"Are you collecting thieves, too?" Agnes asked with a laugh.

"No, but thieves got in here last night and stole a lot of sash weights," Harry said. "They're valuable scrap—I mean sash weights are. We got some red paint clues and maybe we can do some detective work."

"Oh, couldn't we help with that?" asked Agnes impulsively.

"No!" said Buddy decisively. "Well, maybe later," he added as he noted the disappointed look on the girls' faces. "Just now you'll have all you can do fixing up the club house."

"All right," agreed Lucy. And Mary asked:

"May we look at the place they stole the sash weights?"

Buddy kindly pointed out the empty

weight compartments on each side of the
two windows in the Victory Club. He also
showed the red paint splashes and told how
they got there.

"The red paint is a clue," he explained.

"Yes, I understand," remarked his
cousin. "And I guess maybe a chisel would
also be a clue."

"A chisel!" exclaimed Buddy. "What
do you mean?"

"Well," went on Agnes, "you can see
where the thieves cut the sash weight cords
with a chisel. There are the marks against
the wood at the back part of this space
where the sash weights slid up and down.
See!"

She pointed out some straight, deep in-
dentations in the wood.

"Golly! She's right!" exclaimed Buddy.
"I meant to look and see how the sash-
weight cords were cut. That's it. The
thieves had a hammer and chisel.

"They put the sharp edge of the chisel
against a cord, up against the wood. Then
they hit the handle of the chisel with the

hammer and the rope was cut through in a second. That's what made two of the upper sashes fall so suddenly that they woke me up. It's a good clue, Agnes."

"Now can we do detective work for you?" asked Lucy.

"I—I guess so," Buddy answered in a sort of dreamy voice. He was still looking at the chisel marks in the window sash compartments. "Let's take a look at the other side of the garage," he proposed.

The Victory Club members ran out and into the other section of the building. There was no door in the partition between the two rooms. Mr. Martyne had taken out his car during the first meeting of the Victory Club and the admission of the girl members soon afterward.

"Yes, here they are—chisel marks!" Buddy exclaimed.

"Those thieves came well prepared," commented Tom.

"I wonder if they got in other garages," said Harry.

"That's what we have to find out about,"

Buddy said. "I say," he called to the girls, "we'll let you help in this scrap campaign any way you can—detective work or anything—but just now if you'll fix up the place, we'll go down and see the mayor, or somebody, and find out where we can start to collect scrap."

"And find out if other garages were robbed of sash weights," suggested Tom.

"Sure!" Buddy agreed.

"All right," assented the three girls.

As the boys were preparing to leave, they heard, out in the street, a discordant jangle of bells.

"It's a junk man!" cried Tom. "Let's ask him if he bought any sash weights from anybody since last night."

The boys ran out to intercept the junkman. He was driving a bony, dirty white horse hitched to a ramshackle wagon on which was piled parts of old iron beds, a cracked kitchen stove, some auto tires very much worn and other scrap material. Seeing the boys coming toward him, the junkman pulled up his horse and asked:

"You got somethings to sell, please?"

"Do you buy sash weights?" asked Buddy, winking at his chums to let him conduct the inquiry.

"Sesh veights—you mean from vinders?"

"Yes," Buddy nodded.

"Sure I buy dem. Dey is good iron. You got some?"

"We had some," Buddy went on. "They're gone now. But did you buy any today?" He stepped up on the hub of a wheel and looked into the motley collection of scrap.

"No, I didn't get no sash veights. But I buy dem if you have some. Dey's goot scrap."

"Look here," said Tom. "Do you know what this scrap collection is for?"

"Sure I know. It's to halp beat de Excess."

"The Axis—the Japs, the Germans and the Italians who are against this country," said Buddy. "But do you know there's a scrap campaign on in Mountchester now? All scrap has to be turned in to City Hall or

to the Mayor's scrap committee. It's got to
be sold to regular junk dealers. They have
to turn it over to mills and other places the
government picks out. And the money goes
to the U.S.O. or Red Cross. You know you
can't go around buying junk like you did
before."

"Sure, I know," said the junkman smiling. "I'm oddervised."

"Oddervised?" questioned Tom. "What
does he mean?"

"Here, take a looks," said the junkman.
He pulled a somewhat dirty paper from his
pocket. It had become dirty from his grimy
hands, it was evident. But the paper bore
the heading of Mayor Doremus and the
Mountchester municipal seal. It said:

"The bearer, Simon Lasker, is authorized
to buy junk from citizens of Mountchester.
He will pay the market price and the money
he pays is to be turned over to the salvage
committee."

"Oh, you're *authorized!*" said Buddy,
handing back the paper.

"Sure, dat's vot I said—oddervised. You got any sash veights or odder scrap?"

"Not now, but we may have later," said Buddy. "Where's your junk yard?"

"Over in Verona," and he named a small village outside Mountchester. "I come past almost every day. I buy your scrap."

"All right," said Buddy. "And if you happen to buy any sash weights with red paint on 'em, you let us know."

"Sure I vill. But I never see painted sash veights."

"Maybe you will," remarked Buddy significantly. "Keep your eyes open. When did you get this?" he asked handing back the "oddervised" paper.

"Dis mornin'. I hear about the scraps drive so I come over. I'm a citizen," he said proudly. "I got peoples over in Oorup. De Excess killed some of 'em. I get de scraps now to help. You sell me?"

"We sure will!" chorused Buddy and his chums.

"That fellow will help us in our detective

work," Buddy said. "And now let's get on down town to find out the best way to work this campaign. We've got to get in the scrap!"

"And we want to find out if any more garages lost sash weights last night," added Tom as Simon Lasker urged his old white horse down the street to the tune of the jangling bells.

Buddy and his chums hurried on, casting back looks which showed the three girls busy with their plans for decorating the club house.

The three chums were half way down the street when they heard some one shouting after them:

"I say—now—fellows—wait for me—will you—now? I got something to tell you—now—it's great. I—now—I can tell you where—now—there's a lot of it—a lot!"

"Oh, it's Tommie (Now) Tasker," said Buddy looking back.

"Oh, he's a pest," said Harry. "He's too small to help."

"You never can tell," said Buddy. "Let's hear what he has to say. All right, Tommie, what is it?" Buddy asked.

The boy (he was small) was very much in earnest. He had a habit of interjecting "now" into his talk when he was excited. And he was excited at this moment.

"I—now—I can tell you—now—where there's a regular treasure trove—now!" exclaimed Tommie. "I—now—been reading a book—now—a story—it tells about a treasure trove—only that—now—was gold—but this is different."

"What is it?" asked Harry.

"It's a big lot of old—now—iron!" gasped Tommie. "Nobody but me—now—knows where it is. If I show you the treasure trove will—now—you let me join your Victory Club, Buddy?"

The three chums looked at one another and then at Tommie (Now) Tasker.

CHAPTER VI

BUDDY, to whom his two chums were leaving the situation, looked at something Tommie held in one hand.

"What is it?" asked Buddy.

"It's a gear wheel," answered the small boy. "Some of the—now—teeth are busted —but it's a—now—gear wheel."

"Yes, I can see that," admitted Buddy. "Where did you get it?"

"Over at the place where the—now— treasure trove—now—is. I found it—by— now—accident. If I show you can I join the club?"

"How did you hear about any club?" asked Tom.

"I heard—now—Agnes Randall, and your—now sisters," said Tommie, nodding at Tom and Harry. "They were talking about—now—Buddy's Victory Club—"

"I tell you it isn't *my* club!" interrupted the red-haired boy. "It a Victory Club all right—but anybody can join—"

"Then can't I?" burst out Tommie.

"Well, maybe," said Buddy, not having foreseen the little trap into which he had let himself. "But what about the girls?"

"And what about the treasure trove?" asked Tom.

"That's more to the point," said Harry.

"Well, it was like—now—this," said Tommie. "After I found the treasure trove —this—now—is some of it," and he held up the broken gear wheel—"I was going along and I heard the three girls—now—telling about Buddy's—I—now—mean the Victory Club. They said they were going to—now —ask to join but if you—now—wouldn't let 'em they'd make a club of their own. So why can't I—now—join? I'd—now—be a good member."

"I guess you can," laughed Buddy. "Especially if you help us get in a lot of scrap."

"Oh, there's a pile of—now—I mean a

lot of it," said the small boy. "You sure I can join—now—your club, I mean?"

"Oh, sure," said Buddy. "We'll take you to the club house later. But first we have to go down to the mayor's office to find out just how and where and when all this scrap is going to be collected and how we can help with iron and rubber and tin cans. We have to go to the mayor's office first— or maybe to see some of the committee."

"You won't have to," said Tommie.

"Why not?" asked Harry.

"Because it—now—tells all about it here. That's—now—why I went hunting scrap and I—now—I found it. Here—now!" said Tommie.

The small boy held out the issue of the weekly Mountchester Herald. On the front page was an account of the scrap campaign and rules and instructions for committees, sub-committees and individuals to guide them in making scrap collections. Directions were given where to deposit the iron, old rubber tires, tin cans and anything that could help bring the war to a victorious end.

"Say, this is great!" said Buddy as he glanced over the article. "It tells us just what we want to know."

"It'll save us a trip down town," spoke Tom.

"Then we can go see Tommie's treasure trove," suggested Harry.

"If there really is one," remarked Buddy. "Oh, I believe you found some old iron," he was quick to say as he saw the small boy's indignant glance. "But it takes a lot of scrap to make even a small treasure trove."

"There's—now—a lot of it," said Tommie. "A heap of a lot! I found it by accident. If you're—now—sure I'm in the club I'll take you to the place where—now—it is."

"Oh, you're in the club," promised Buddy. He remembered how once, about a year ago, when he, Tom and Harry were fishing without much luck, Tommie showed them a little-known spot where they pulled

out some big ones. Buddy thought Tommie
might be a repeater.

"Well, let's go," suggested Harry.

"I hope," said Tom as the four walked
along, "that Tommie's treasure trove
doesn't turn out to be some of your sash
weights, Buddy."

"How could they be?" asked the red-
haired lad.

"Well, the thieves might have hidden
them, with others they stole last night, and
Tommie might have found them."

"What's that?" asked the small boy who
was looking at his gear wheel sample.

"Thieves got in Buddy's garage last
night, and stole all the sash weights," said
Tom.

"And we're going to do detective work
and find 'em," added Harry.

"My—now—treasure trove isn't sash
weights," said Tommie. "It's lots bigger
pieces of—now—iron than that. But a—
now—lot of sash weights were stolen last
night."

"How do you know?" asked Buddy.

"It's now—in the paper," said the small boy. "I bought the paper—now—when I went to the store for my mother. On—now —page two—I mean about the sash weights."

Buddy flipped open the paper. There was the item. It stated that just as the paper was going to press it was learned from the police that a number of garages had been entered recently and sash weights cut loose from their cords.

"Well, then the thieves must have been busy before last night," said Tom Gordon.

"They could be," said Buddy. "This scrap campaign has been talked about for several weeks. Everybody knew we had to get in a lot of scrap iron, and sash weights are right up that alley. Well, now that we have all the directions we need, let's get on to Tommie's treasure trove. You lead the way, Tommie."

"Sure—now—I will."

"And as long as you're a club member,"

suggested Harry, "you might as well tell us where you're taking us to this big store of old iron."

"Sure, I'll tell you," assented the small boy. "It's the old—now—stove factory down by Patton Creek."

"That!" exclaimed Tom. "Why, that's been closed, abandoned and in ruins these last five years."

"There's nothing in that factory," said Buddy, in somewhat disappointed tones. "No use going there. I looked in when I first heard about the scrap campaign, but there's not so much as a piece of old iron pipe in the factory."

"It isn't—now—exactly *in* the old stove factory," said Tommie. "I found the iron treasure trove in a sort of—now—dump outside—covered—now—with dirt. Must have been there a long—now—while 'cause it's all rusty."

"That won't hurt the scrap," said Harry. "Half of it the junkmen get is rusty. Say, maybe Tommie has something after all."

"Sure—now—I have!" declared the small boy. "I'll—now—show you! Come on!"

It took them about ten minutes to reach the abandoned factory. It formerly turned out old style kitchen cooking stoves. But with the coming of gas, the cook stove business fell off and the factory was abandoned.

"It's around—now—to the back," explained Tommie as he led the way. "I'm glad I found it—now—this treasure trove. And I'm—now—glad I belong to your club, Buddy. Come around—now—this way—"

Tommie stopped suddenly in his tracks and ceased speaking.

"What's the matter?" asked Buddy.

"Look who's—now—sneaking around here!" whispered the small boy.

CHAPTER VII

THE LONELY HUT

MADE cautious by Tommie's signal for silence, Buddy and his two chums grew silent and, also silently, moved up close to the small boy. They stood in one of the work rooms of the old stove factory. From there they could look out on an embankment which went down to the edge of Patton Creek.

"The—now—treasure trove of old scrap iron—now—is in that bank," whispered Tommie. "But I'm afraid those—now—other fellows are going to get it ahead of us."

"Not much they won't!" declared Buddy, also in a whisper.

"Who are they?" asked Tom. He was back of the others and could not see very well.

"You could almost guess who," said Buddy. "It's Sid Monson, Ike Blatter and Jake Turner. Keep still, let's see what they're up to."

Buddy's club members did not have long to wait. It seemed that Jake and his gang had only arrived a few minutes previous. They appeared to be on a sort of scouting mission. For Jake said:

"Well, we've looked all through this dump. There's nothing here."

"Not even sash weights," said Ike.

"Shut up! Somebody might hear you!" cautioned Sid.

Buddy and his chums had heard, and Tom gave Harry a poke in the ribs to call his attention to this remark. Tom poked so hard, though not intending to, that Harry grunted.

"What's that?" exclaimed Ike, looking up from where he stood on the edge of Tommie's treasure trove.

"Oh, nothing. Just a stray dog or cat, I guess," said Jake.

"Well, all right. But don't talk so free," cautioned Sid. "You never know who may hear you. But I guess there isn't any scrap here. We might as well—"

Suddenly his foot slipped on the shelving hill of dirt and he went down, grasping at anything he could reach. It happened to be a half-buried pipe. Sid's sliding fall exposed the pipe and with it a lot of other old iron scrap that had been buried with it.

"Say, would you look at that!" cried Ike.

"Wow! What a pile of old iron!" added Jake. "We can get a lot of money for this. Let's pull it out and get our junkman to come for it." He stepped down toward Sid and began delving into the treasure trove. But Sid, who seemed to be the leader of the three cronies, stopped him and said:

"Leave this just as it is. We can't take it away. And if we uncover it somebody else will see it before we can get the junkman here. Let's cover it up and leave it."

"Leave it?" objected Ike.

"I mean for a little while. We'll go get

the junkman and come back before night. Wow, what a find this is!"

"See! Didn't I—now—tell you!" whispered Tommie to his friends.

"Quiet!" cautioned Buddy. "Stoop down, fellows, so they won't see us," he added.

But Sid and his gang were too busy scraping dirt with their hands and feet to cover up the scrap Sid's fall had revealed. The three outside the old factory were so busy that Buddy and his chums had a chance to move to one of the inner rooms where they were well hidden.

There they heard the three depart, to go, probably, after the junkman who might come, in an hour or two, and gather all the scrap.

"Well, this is a nice thing—not!" exclaimed Tom.

"To think of those bad eggs getting ahead of us this way!" said Harry.

"They haven't gotten ahead of us yet!" declared Buddy.

"What are you going to—now—do?"
asked Tommie. "Are they going to—now—
get the credit of turning in the scrap I
found?"

"Not much!" said Buddy. "We'll turn
it in ourselves, which is something Sid and
his gang don't intend to do."

"You mean they plan to take this scrap
and sell it and keep the money?" asked
Harry.

"That's what I think," was the red-
haired boy's answer. "Only they're not going to get away with it. Not any more than
the thieves did who took our sash weights."

"Do you think these fellows did that?"
asked Tom.

"I don't want to accuse anybody until
I'm sure," said Buddy. "We heard them
talk of sash weights, but maybe it didn't
mean what we think. Anyhow, we'll stop
this game of theirs and do some more detective work on the sash-weight case."

"What are you going to do?" asked
Harry.

"Cut back to City Hall," said Buddy, "and tell the mayor, or some member of the salvage committee, to send a truck out here to pick up this scrap. We don't need to say anything about Sid and his gang if we get the scrap out first. We can do that. And I'd like to see the faces of these three when they come and find the treasure trove gone. Ha! Ha!"

"Ha! Ha!" echoed Buddy's chums.

"Come on!" the red-haired boy called. "We can't waste any time!"

"But look," objected Tommie. "If we go away and—now—leave this scrap, maybe those fellows will—now—come back and get it."

"That's so," admitted Buddy. "I didn't think of that. Here's what we'll do. I'll go back to City Hall with Tommie. It's his find and he ought to get credit for it."

"Sure!" agreed Tom and Harry.

"I can show the mayor this gear wheel," said the small boy. "I can tell him how I was—now—just scouting around and how I saw a little piece of scrap and how I—now —dug and found more and came and—now —told you boys and joined the—now— club.''

''Correct!'' laughed Buddy. ''It's your party, Tommie. You and I will go see the mayor, or somebody who can send out a truck before that double-crossing junkman gets here.''

''Do you think it's the same one we saw?'' asked Tom.

''You mean Simon Lasker?'' asked Buddy. ''No, I don't. I think he is a square shooter. This must be the one that the sash-weight thieves deal with. We'll soon find out.''

''What do you want Harry and me to do?'' asked Tom.

''Stay here on guard,'' answered Buddy.

''What if those fellows come back before you come with the salvage truck, Buddy?'' asked Harry.

''Just warn Sid and his gang that if they take out one piece of junk we'll report 'em to the salvage committee and the Red Cross and the U.S.O. and everybody in town," said Buddy. "That'll scare 'em off. No junkman, even if he wants to go in a crooked deal, will dare buy junk when he knows he's going to be found out. You aren't afraid to stay here, are you?"

"I should say not!" declared Tom.

"We can deal with Sid and his bunch!" asserted Harry.

"Come on then, Tommie!" invited Buddy and the two set off on the run.

Left to themselves, Tom and Harry wandered about the old factory. It was a deserted, lonesome place, seldom visited, now that it had fallen into ruin. The two watchers went outside and, by kicking away some of the dirt, disclosed that quite a substantial pile of scrap lay beneath it.

"They must have dumped a lot of discarded machinery and parts here for a long time—I mean the factory workers did," said Tom.

"That's about it," agreed Harry. "And

bits of broken or defective castings, too,"
he added as he kicked aside some gear
wheels like the one Tommie had shown.

"Must be a couple of tons of old iron
here," went on Tom.

"All of that," said Harry. "It would
make a neat little lot of spending money for
Sid's gang if they got it."

"They won't get it," said Tom. "Of
course the scrap would go into the war, just
the same, but it would be cheating for those
fellows to take the money for themselves."

"Sure," agreed Harry. "And I guess a
junkman who would buy bootleg scrap, so to
speak, wouldn't pay the highest price."

"Probably not," said Tom. "Well, let's
take a walk around. Neither Buddy nor the
other bunch can be back here inside of an
hour."

The two chums strolled about the old factory. Once it had been operated by water
power from Patton Creek, but in later years
a steam engine had furnished motive power.
Part of the old wooden power wheel, turned

by water coming over a dam, was in place. But all machinery and the steam engine had long since been removed from the ruined plant.

As Tom and Harry were walking along the stream, still keeping in view the old factory, they saw, down in a sort of hollow near the old flume, a small wooden shack. It was about six feet square and not much more in height, and seemed to have been made from boards from the old mill race and wheel.

"I didn't know that was here," said Tom in a low voice.

"Neither did I," said Harry. "Let's take a look. Maybe it's a hideout for Sid and his gang."

As the two boys approached the lonely hut, they were surprised to see a shabbily-dressed man dart out of it and slink away through the bushes.

CHAPTER VIII

SOMETHING SUSPICIOUS

FOR a moment Tom and Harry were too
surprised to say anything or do anything. They had not expected to see anyone
in or near the mysterious little hut. But
as the man disappeared in the underbrush,
Tom asked:

"What do you know about that?"

"I don't know what to think," admitted
Harry. "He looked like a tramp."

"That's what he was, I guess," agreed
Tom. "This shack is just a tramp's hideout. What say we go take a look in?"

"Might as well. That is, if there aren't
some other tough customers in the hut."

Harry and Tom cautiously approached
the lonely hut. No sounds came from it and
there were no signs of any human inhabit-
ants. But the boys did not approach too
fast.

"They may be hiding there waiting for us," suggested Tom.

"That's right," agreed Harry. "That one fellow may have run out just to bait us so we'd come closer."

"You mean so they might jump out and grab us?" asked Tom. He hardly expected his chum to agree with him, but that's just what happened.

"Sure they might," said Harry. "We got to be careful."

"But who—what—I mean why would anybody want to hide out in this lonely shack and catch us?" Tom inquired coming to a sudden halt.

"They might be fifth columnists—saboteurs, maybe. We have to be on the alert for them."

"You mean Japs?"

"Not likely to be Japs around here. They'd be too easy to spot. But they might be Nazi Germans. A lot of them pretend to be good United States citizens but on the side they're working for Hitler. Some of them might have set up some sort of a secret station here.''

"It's secret all right," agreed Tom. "I don't believe many persons around here know of it. We just stumbled on it. I think we ought to see what's inside it and if there's anyone there.''

"Sure," agreed Harry.

The two boys once more continued their cautious approach. There was still no sound and no indication of life in the lonely hut. But suddenly there came from it a thumping noise as if something had fallen with a thud.

"What was that?" whispered Tom.

"You know as much as I do about it," replied his chum.

There was a rustling of scurrying feet over dead leaves and a moment later, out of the makeshift door of the hut, ran a brown creature with a long tail.

"A rat!" cried Harry.

"A big water rat," added Tom with a

laugh. "Gosh, but it gave me a scare for a moment."

"Same here," agreed his chum. Then, as he watched the rat scurry for the creek, Harry asked: "Why do you think that rat was in the hut?"

"Maybe he lives there," said Tom. "No, that couldn't be. Water rats have their burrows in holes along the creek bank. But maybe he was the pet of that man who ran out."

"You mean the Nazi spy?"

"If he was a Nazi spy—yes."

"Then there were two of a kind in the shack," chuckled Harry. "I mean two rats. But I guess this shows there aren't any more persons in there. Our coming so close scared the rat and he ran out."

"Let's go up and look in then," suggested Tom.

"I wish Buddy were here," said Harry. "He'd know what to do."

"Well, we can wait until Buddy and Tom-

mie come back—probably with some of the
salvage committee," said Tom. "But I
don't believe there's any danger now. And
if we could look in the hut, and, maybe, find
a hidden Nazi machine gun—"

"Oh, cut out the funny business!"
laughed Harry. "It won't be anything like
that. But maybe this is a hideout for some
fifth column Nazi workers. Anyhow, let's
take a look."

Satisfied that the departure of the water
rat indicated that the hut was now probably
deserted, the two boys approached it more
rapidly. They could see it had been recently
constructed from odds and ends of wood
from the old water wheel, and parts of the
abandoned factory.

There was a door to the shack, though it
was hung rather askew on rusty hinges.
There was also a window which opened on
the creek side. The door was open and the
boys were soon peering through and gazing
about the hut.

A quick glance showed it contained two

chairs, a sort of bench or table, some boxes and a lantern. On the bench was a pasteboard box, which had been wrapped in newspapers. And as soon as the boys saw this, part of the mystery was explained.

"That man who ran away was eating his lunch in here," decided Tom.

"And he ran away, when we came, without finishing," added Harry.

"And then the rat came up out of the creek and was having his lunch from the man's lunch when we disturbed the second rat," went on Tom.

"You still think that man was a Nazi spy?" asked Harry.

"Maybe. But it doesn't matter. He's gone and I guess the water rat didn't leave much of the lunch. There's nothing more here. We might as well go back to the factory and that pile of scrap. Buddy may come along any minute and he'll wonder where we are."

"Hadn't we better report this shack to somebody?" asked Harry.

"Yes, I think we should.   To the police or the defense committee or the mayor or somebody."

"We'll tell Buddy first and hear what he says," suggested Harry.

"Yes, I guess that's the best thing to do," assented Tom.

They were about to leave the hut, after having stepped inside to get a better view, when Harry suddenly exclaimed:

"Hark! Do you hear that?"

"Hear what?"

"A sort of ticking—like a clock."

Tom cocked his head on one side in order to listen better.

"The creek water makes such a noise that's about all I can hear," he said. "Keep still a second."

Both boys stood motionless. And then, above the murmur of the creek over its stony bed, they both heard a faint ticking.

"Infernal machine!" cried Tom. "A bomb! Let's run!"

He darted out of the hut doorway in such

a hurry that he spun his chum around. This movement pushed Harry further into the hut and up against the table or bench. The package of food was jostled and out of the paper wrapping tumbled a small alarm clock. It was ticking away industriously.

"What a scare!" laughed Tom as he turned back when Harry called.

"It had us both fooled," agreed Harry. "But," he went on, "if somebody hangs out here with his lunch and an alarm clock, it means more than just a tramp."

"I think it does," agreed his chum. "We'll report this."

"First we'll tell Buddy," decided Harry. "We can talk it over at the club meeting to-night. Hark!" he said again.

A shout came to them from up on the bank where stood the deserted stove factory.

CHAPTER IX

FOILED

HARRY and Tom paused in their retreat from the hut.

Again came the shout:

"It's Buddy!" exclaimed Tom.

"Sure enough!" agreed Harry. "He's wondering what has happened to us. We ought to have been back there—up at the scrap pile."

"But we haven't wasted any time," said Tom. "We've made a discovery, though I can't quite figure it all out."

"We'll have to get Buddy to do some of his detective work on it," said Harry. "He'll be surprised at this. Yes! Hello! We're coming!" he shouted as Buddy hailed again.

The two were climbing the embankment up to the old factory and the scrap pile when they were startled by a movement in the underbrush back of them, in the direction of the hut.

"Maybe that tramp or Nazi is coming back," said Tom.

"Or maybe the water rat. But we'd better go up and see what Buddy wants. Maybe he's in trouble."

Another loud shout from the leader of the Victory Club seemed to indicate that he was at least impatient. For Buddy called:

"Tom! Harry! Where in the world are you?"

"Coming!" shouted Tom.

"Right away!" added Harry. "We've made a discovery!"

"Well, Tommie's discovery of this big scrap pile has to be taken care of first," called Buddy. "So come running!"

Which Harry and Tom began to do. But first they looked back in the direction of the sound in the bushes. And they saw, coming along a side road that was seldom used, a ramshackle junk wagon on which, besides the driver, sat Sid Monson, Jake Turner and Ike Blatter. The driver was urging along a brown and more spritely horse than the bony white nag the boys had seen Simon Lasker driving.

"It's another junkman," said Tom.

"Sid and his gang went and got him to take away this scrap, or some of it," added Harry.

"But they're going to be fooled!" chuckled Tom.

The two hurried on up the hill to where Buddy waited for them near the scrap pile. Another look back seemed to indicate that Sid and his two cronies had not seen Tom and Harry.

"What were you doing down there?" asked Buddy. "I thought you were supposed to guard the scrap pile."

"We were," said Tom. "We didn't go very far away."

"And we found something that'll open your eyes," went on Harry.

"Maybe," admitted the red-haired club leader. "But if Sid and his gang had come and taken this scrap while you two were down fishing in the creek, that would have opened your eyes."

"We weren't fishing," said Tom.

"But you aren't back any too soon," said Harry, looking at Buddy, Tommie and a city refuse truck which had pulled up near the scrap pile.

"What do you mean?" asked Buddy.

"Sid and his gang are coming up that side road with a junkman," said Harry. "You're only just in time to fool him."

"Oh, we'll fool him all right," laughed Buddy. "This is Mr. Bart, chairman of the Mountchester Salvage Committee," said Buddy introducing his two chums.

"Hello, boys," greeted Mr. Bart. "This is quite a discovery you have made—all this fine scrap. None of our committee knew about it."

"Tommie discovered it," said Buddy.

"Yes, so I understand," went on Mr. Bart. "He will receive the formal thanks of the committee."

"Oh, I—now—I don't want any—now—thanks," said Tommie, blushing. "I'm—now—glad to do it. And Buddy let me in his club—now—on account of it."

"What club is that?" asked Mr. Bart.

"It's Buddy's—" began Tom.

"It's just a Victory Club a lot of us boys —and some girls—got up to help in this scrap salvage drive," interrupted Buddy.

"Splendid!" exclaimed Mr. Bart. "It's a good, patriotic gesture. Well now, men," he said to the driver on the refuse truck and two helpers he had with him, "pile in and get out the scrap."

"Before somebody else takes it," said Tom.

"Why, who else would take it?" asked Mr. Bart.

"Sid Monson and his gang are on their way here," said Buddy. He quickly explained about the other group of boys and added: "I don't say but what they would turn the scrap over to a junk dealer and, in

time, it would go to help make planes, tanks
and guns for victory. But—"

"I understand what you mean," interrupted Mr. Bart. "We don't want any
double handling of the scrap if we can help
it. Speed is very necessary in this war. I
will tell this other crowd that we are taking
care of this scrap—if they come after it."

"Oh, they're coming," said Tom.

"Here they are now!" exclaimed Buddy.
He pointed to the side road which emerged
from a clump of trees just beyond the old
stove factory. From the thicket rattled the
junk wagon with the three cronies aboard.

"Hey you!" yelled Sid when he saw
Buddy and his friends standing near the
city refuse truck. "That's our scrap!
Leave it alone!"

"Your scrap?" asked Mr. Bart as he
stepped into view. "I understood that all
scrap discovered, or turned in, was the prop-
erty of the Mountchester Salvage Committee, of which I happen to be chairman."

"Oh," said Sid, dubiously. "I—I didn't know that."

"I'm telling you," said Mr. Bart, pointedly. "These city employes will take charge of this scrap. It will go to an authorized junkman. Are you authorized to collect scrap?" Mr. Bart asked the driver of the junk wagon.

"Not specially," said the man in surly tones. "But these boys came after me and said they had a lot of scrap and that I could get it and turn it in. That's what I was going to do."

"I don't doubt that," said Mr. Bart. "You would have to turn the scrap in to get your money for it. I suppose these boys offered to sell you the scrap."

"No we didn't!" quickly cried Sid. Buddy saw him give the junk wagon driver a secret nudge to keep quiet. "We just told him where it was. If he gave us the money we would have turned it in."

"I am glad to hear you say so," spoke Mr. Bart.

"Sure, that's the way it was," spoke the junkman. "I don't make much off this scrap after I have to cart it and sort and take it to a big wholesale dealer. But I'll do my part."

"I'm sure you will," said Mr. Bart, smiling. "But I'm sorry to say you have had this trip for nothing. The city will pick up this scrap directly and send it to an authorized wholesale dealer."

"But don't we get any credit for finding it and offering to turn it in?" asked Ike.

"We found it first," grumbled Jake Turner.

"Oh, you did not!" cried Tommie. "I—now—found it and I told Buddy and he—now—put me in his club. I—now—found the scrap first; didn't I, Buddy?"

"You sure did!" said the red-haired boy. "You're too late, Sid. Maybe you can find some sash weights if you look in some other garages."

"What do you mean by that crack?" cried Sid. He and his cronies were several years older than Buddy and his chums, though, by reason of little application to their lessons, they were in Buddy's class at school.

"What do you mean, Martyne?"

"Oh, I just happened to mention sash weights," went on Buddy with an innocent face. "But if you find any—look out for red paint."

"Red paint!" cried Jake.

"Yes, red paint," went on Buddy. He told his chums afterward he was sure the junkman shot a quick look at the three cronies. But that had to do with some detective work done later.

"Get into the scrap, men!" called Mr. Bart to the city workers.

"We can't take this all in one load," said the foreman.

"No, I don't expect you to. I think it will take three trips, by the size of this old iron," said Mr. Bart estimating the old factory scrap dump.

"But if they go away," said Tommie,

"those other fellows—now—may take the—now—scrap and—"

"They won't take it," said the foreman with a chuckle. "I'll leave a man here on guard. Come on, get busy!" he called to his helpers.

As they began to shovel away the dirt and expose the old pipes, broken gear wheels, parts of stoves and other iron, Sid and his cronies climbed into the other wagon and drove away.

"We fooled 'em," said Buddy. And then, as he felt very elated, he jumped into the air and clicked his heels together three times.

CHAPTER X

ON THE TRAIL

HAVING performed his little heel-clicking trick, Buddy was ready to give some attention to Tom and Harry. The city's men were busy getting out the scrap.

"How much you think is there?" asked Tommie.

"Must be all of five tons," said the foreman. "It's as thick as plums in a Christmas pudding."

"Five tons!" exclaimed Tommie. "That's—now—a lot of scrap; isn't it—now—I mean?"

"It sure is, now and always," said Buddy. "You did a good job, Tommie. The club is proud of you. And now what's this discovery you and Tom made, Harry?"

"It may be something, or it may be nothing," Tom said.

"Come and take a look," invited Harry.

Leaving the city men to get out the scrap, Buddy and his chums descended the hill to the edge of the creek. They could see Sid Monson and his cronies, aboard the disappointed junkman's wagon, clattering out of sight along the side road.

Harry and Tom showed Buddy and Tommie the strange hut. It was still as silent and deserted as when the two discoverers had first seen it and watched the water rat run out.

"What do you make of it, Buddy?" asked Tom.

"Looks like a tramps' hangout."

"That's what we thought first," said Harry. "But I'm not so sure."

"Would you say tramps carry an alarm clock around with them?" asked Tom.

"Not as a rule," Buddy admitted. "They don't generally care whether they get up early or not—unless, I suppose, they want to catch a freight train out of town. Where's this alarm clock?"

"In the shack," said Tom.

"Come and have a listen," urged Harry.

The hut was somewhat crowded when the four boys stood in it. Buddy looked at what remained of the lunch on the bench and said it hadn't been there long. It showed evidence of having been gnawed by the rat.

"I think the man who ran out was eating as we came along," said Tom.

"And when he left the water rat came in for his share," said Harry. "The question is, Buddy, what was the man doing in the shack?"

Buddy was looking sharply around. He peered under the bench which was made by some planks nailed across two boxes. The bench seemed solid and heavy when Buddy tried to move it.

"Feels as if those boxes held something heavy—like metal," said the red-haired boy.

"Maybe some more scrap iron," suggested Tommie. "If it is—now—we ought to take it—now—out."

"It isn't likely anybody would nail up scrap iron in boxes just to make them heavy

to help hold up a bench," said Buddy. "But
these boxes may once have been in the old
factory and have held parts of machinery.
When they were thrown out with other
scrap, after the factory was abandoned,
some tramp may have picked them up and
used them as part of his dining room table."

"But this hut hasn't been here long,"
argued Tom. "Of course I don't often get
down this way. But from the looks of it,
Buddy, wouldn't you say it was made recently?"

"Not more than a month," was Buddy's
opinion. "But tramps could have made it.
This place isn't far from the railroad, you
know, and tramps go and come by freight
trains, mostly."

"Do you think we ought to open the boxes
that make up this bench or table?" asked
Harry.

"Not now," said the red-haired boy. "In
the first place they're tightly nailed or
screwed shut. And we haven't anything to
open them with. Besides, we might get

caught doing it. That man might come back."

"And this place isn't ours," said Tom. "I guess it belongs to whoever still owns the old stove factory. Maybe we haven't any right to take that scrap for the club's salvage drive."

"We'll take a chance on that," said Buddy. "Anyhow, the scrap is being taken officially by the chairman of the salvage committee. That lets us out. But if we go opening boxes that don't belong to us, that's something else."

"It's a sort of mystery I'd like to see solved," spoke Tom.

"So would I," added Harry.

"Well, we'll make this one of the objects of our club," said Buddy. "And that reminds me—we'd better get back and see how the girls are getting along with their curtains and other decorations. We can come here some other day."

"Do you think Sid Monson and his gang

have anything to do with this place?" asked Tom.

"They might have," Buddy admitted. "That's something else we'll have to look into. But first I want to get on the trail of those sash-weight thieves."

"You mean now?" asked Harry.

"No. Not for a few days. Let's get the club going. We need new members. And there's one thing we can sort of take over as our share of the salvage work. I mean something in particular. Mr. Bart told me about it when Tommie went to tell him about this scrap pile."

"What's that?" inquired Tom and Harry.

"Tin can salvage," Buddy explained. "I'll tell you more later. But it seems a lot of tin is needed to help win the war. The Japs have cut off most of our supply by taking over the mines in the Dutch East Indies. So we've got to depend a lot on the tin that can be melted off tin cans."

"Can very much tin be salvaged that way?" asked Tom.

"About one per cent of the weight of a tin can is pure tin," said Buddy. "That isn't much. It takes an awful pile of tin cans to make a pound of tin. But tin is valuable. I think the price is now around $1,200 a ton—I mean it's worth that at the scrap factory. But it's worth a lot more in the war effort."

"You mean you want our club to help collect tin cans?" asked Harry.

"Partly that," said Buddy. "Also we've got to start a sort of educational campaign. Tin cans have to be processed by people who empty them in their homes. It isn't enough to just put out empty tin cans for the salvage collectors. They've got to be processed, and a lot of families aren't doing that. Mr. Bart said we could help in that way."

"How do you 'process' an empty tin can?" asked Tom.

"I—now—know!" exclaimed Tommie.

"You got to—now—step on it and flatten it —now—out."

"That's only part of it," said Buddy. "We'll take that up at our next club meeting which will be tonight—that is if the girls have the curtains up. And it's up to you fellows to get some new members. Bring them tonight and I'll tell you about the tin can collection."

"May I—now—come to this meeting— now—I mean?" asked Tommie.

"Sure, you're a member of the Victory Club in good standing," said Buddy with a laugh. "Well, let's get back home."

Satisfied that the taking out of the scrap from the old factory was well and safely under way, Buddy and his chums hurried back to Mountchester. They found the three girls had not only put up the curtains in the garage club house, but had brought in some rugs, another table, more chairs, some pictures and two lamps.

"Say, you made this place look swell!" exclaimed Buddy.

"Aren't you glad you let us join?" asked Agnes.

"We sure are!" declared Tom.

"You girls are expected at the meeting tonight," said Buddy. "Bring some other girls if you like. They can belong. We'll need a lot of members to get in all the scrap —especially tin cans."

"We have a lot of cans at our house," said Lucy. "Mother doesn't know what to do with them. She started saving them after she read about the Japs getting all our tin."

"We'll talk about tin cans tonight, and how to process them," said Buddy. "There's a lot of things to do."

It was now late in the afternoon. The girls put some finishing touches to their first efforts at decorating the club house. Then they left, promising to come back that evening with several new members.

Tom, Harry and Tommie also started to leave, promising to return with recruits for the Victory Club.

"Well, we've made a start," said Buddy as he walked down the street with Tom and Harry who were on their way home.

"Where are you going?" Tom asked his red-haired chum.

"Down to City Hall."

"What for?" Harry wanted to know.

"Oh, I want to get on the trail of the sash-weight thieves and also the junkman who bought them."

"How can you find out at City Hall?" asked Tom.

"I'm not sure I can," said Buddy, somewhat mysteriously. "But the trail may start there."

CHAPTER XI

A DISCOVERY

WHAT Buddy found out at City Hall, and whether he got on the trail there, was not at once made known to his two special chums. For there was so much to do at the first real meeting of the Victory Club that Buddy had no time to talk about his mysterious errand.

There was scarcely room in the garage club house for all the new, prospective members who assembled there after supper. The three girls each brought a friend. Tommie brought three chums, somewhat his own age. Tom Gordon had four recruits and Harry Clee topped that with five.

"I didn't really bring any new members," said Buddy when he had called the meeting to order. "But I telephoned some fellows and they said they'd come."

There was a knock at the side of the club house section of the garage, the big doors of which were open as the night was hot.

"Maybe these are some of your new members, Buddy," said Tom.

"Well, I'd esteem it an honor to belong to this club," said a voice as Mr. Bart stepped in. "But I fear I am too old. However, I come as Buddy's guest."

"Thank you," spoke Buddy. "I invited Mr. Bart," the red-haired boy went on, speaking to the club members, "to tell us something about the salvage campaign—especially the tin can end of it. That's very important, isn't it, Mr. Bart?"

"Very important, Buddy. Mountchester isn't getting—in fact the nation generally isn't getting—all the tin it should from old cans. There are enough of them, but householders, and others, are careless and neglectful on this point. Buddy thought if I told you more about it, and let you know how important it is, we might get better results."

"I know Mr. Bart can tell you a lot better than I could," said Buddy. "That's why I went to City Hall this afternoon to invite him."

"Is that the trail you went on?" asked Tom in a whisper.

"No, it was another one. I'll tell you later," Buddy replied.

Mr. Bart was now speaking to the members of the Victory Club. He told them about the scrap collection drive in general. He spoke of the need of scrap iron especially.

"About half the new steel that is turned out of our rolling mills in this country comes from old or scrap iron," said the salvage chairman. "The other half is of newly-mined iron ore. Both are important.

"Also important scrap is old rubber, old rope and old papers. These are comparatively easy to locate, collect and send on to the proper salvage mills. We need a lot of old rubber. The Japs captured most of the new rubber supply so we'll have to depend on old scrap for a while."

"But we'll beat those—now—Japs!" exclaimed a shrill, small voice. There was laughter and Mr. Bart said:

"Indeed we will, Tommie Tasker. If not now, soon."

There was more laughter at this mention of Tommie's peculiarity in using the word "now" but Mr. Bart added:

"I think you should all know that Tommie, by a fortunate discovery, has put Mountchester in the way of reaching and, perhaps, exceeding its quota on scrap iron."

He spoke briefly of the discovery by Tommie of the big pile of scrap at the old stove factory and went on:

"I have been informed the scrap from there will run about eight tons. It was splendid work, Tommie."

"Well, Buddy and the other boys helped," said loyal Tommie. There was more laughter and applause.

"I didn't know we had a quota on scrap iron," said Buddy.

"Yes, we have. It's one hundred and fifty tons," said Mr. Bart.

"What's a quota?" asked Fannie Lesser, one of the new girls.

"It means the amount set by the state salvage committee that this little city has to raise," explained Mr. Bart. "But if we have our iron quota in sight, I cannot say as much for our tin quota. That has been set at one hundred tons of old tin cans. This means about one ton of pure tin. The remainder will be scrap steel, for that's what tin cans are made of, thin sheets of steel coated with pure tin."

"Why can't we reach our tin quota? I mean why does it look as if we might not?" asked Buddy.

"Because the people who have the tin cans are too lazy or too indifferent to process them," said Mr. Bart.

"What's process?" asked the girl who had inquired about quota.

"It means putting the tin cans through several operations before you set them out at the curb to be collected, or toss them into the scrap bin we have built at City Hall," said Mr. Bart.

"As soon as a tin can is emptied of its peaches, pears or whatever came in it, the can should be washed, the bottom and top should be cut out evenly and cleanly, and then the paper label removed from the can. Next put the top and bottom pieces inside the tin can cylinder and step on it to flatten it. This will hold the top and bottom in place. That's what processing a tin can means. The flattened can takes up very little space and is easy to de-tin when it reaches the de-tinning factory."

"And what happens there?" asked Buddy.

"Well, it's quite a complicated series of more processes," said Mr. Bart. "First the flattened cans are thoroughly washed. They are put in big, wooden vats and given a good cleaning. Then they go in a chemical bath which takes off the lacquer if there is any. After that the cans are put in other chemical baths which remove the thin, tin coating. The tin is made into ingots and goes to factories which make guns, tanks, planes and other war material. The steel part of the cans goes to the steel mills where it is dumped into furnaces, mixed with iron ore and finally becomes a big gun for victory."

Mr. Bart paused. The club members applauded him and Tom asked:

"Just where are the folks who put out tin cans falling down on the job?"

"They either put out unflattened cans, they don't take off the labels or they don't cut out the tops and bottoms," said Mr. Bart. "Many householders throw their cans, with just the top opened, into the garbage or ash pails. We can't salvage them from there. That's why we're falling behind in our tin quota."

"What do you want our club to do to help?" asked Buddy.

"First, I think perhaps you could tell all

your families and friends how to process tin cans," answered Mr. Bart. "You might, if you have the time, offer to collect unprocessed tin cans from householders and flatten them out yourselves."

"That's just what we'll do!" exclaimed Buddy. "All in favor of this club processing tin cans stand up," he called in a loud voice.

"What about those of us who are already standing?" asked Ned Landerman. There were many unable to find chairs.

"Raise your hands or yell," suggested Buddy.

Instantly there was a small thicket of waving hands and such a shout in the garage that Lola Wagg came running out to see what was the matter.

"We've just decided to process tin cans," Buddy told her.

But when Mrs. Martyne inquired of her maid what all the excitement was about, Lola said:

"Oh, they just decided to address a lot of

tin cans. I guess they're goin' to send 'em
to the soldiers."

"What a strange idea for Buddy's club,"
murmured Mrs. Martyne. But she understood and laughed when, later, her red-
haired son explained.

Mr. Bart left soon after giving details of
the tin can scrap collections and then Buddy
and his fellow club members did some club
business. They elected Buddy president,
though he declared he was willing to step
aside for anyone else. But they wouldn't
have it.

Tom Gordon was elected vice president,
Harry Clee was made secretary with Agnes
Randall as his assistant and Ned Landerman was chosen treasurer. This was a good
choice, Buddy said, as Ned had studied
bookkeeping.

"But I didn't know this club was formed
to make money," Ned remarked.

"It isn't," said Buddy. "We'll get some
money, though, from selling old iron, rubber and tin cans to junk dealers—author-

ized dealers," he was quick to add. "And this money we are going to whack up with the Red Cross and the U.S.O."

"Oh, now I get it," said the treasurer.

Other club details were arranged and then, filled with juvenile enthusiasm about their affairs, the members adjourned, to meet again in a week or whenever Buddy sent out a call.

"Well," remarked Tom as he, Harry and Buddy were the only members remaining in the club house, "it went off pretty well."

"It was swell!" exclaimed Buddy. "Wait a second, fellows!"

He leaped up and clicked his heels three times as he ran his fingers through his red hair, which was standing up enough as it was.

"Maybe you can now tell us what else you did at City Hall late this afternoon, besides getting Mr. Bart to come and talk," said Tom.

"I can," said Buddy. "I made a discovery and I think we are going to make an-

other one tomorrow. First, I discovered
that the junkman Sid and his gang brought
to take away the old factory scrap isn't authorized to do this work.''

"How'd you discover that?'' asked
Harry.

"I noticed the number on the side of his
wagon. All junk dealers have to be licensed
at the County Clerk's office. Each one is
given a number he fastens on his wagon. I
saw this number, and checked at City Hall
where they have on file all the numbers of
junk dealers in the county. This one isn't
authorized to collect victory scrap.''

"Why?'' asked Tom.

"I don't know,'' answered Buddy, "unless it's because he was investigated and it
was found he wasn't on the level.''

"It's just the kind of a junk man Sid and
his gang would pick out,'' commented Tom.

"Sure,'' said Harry.

"Well, maybe,'' Buddy admitted. "We
won't make any accusations until we make

some more discoveries.   And that's what
we're going to try to do tomorrow.''

"How?" asked his chums.

"By taking a little trip on our bikes to
Prattville.   That's where this junk dealer,
Lou Farrish has his place,'' said Buddy.
"We'll get in his junk yard and see if we
can discover any sash weights with red
paint on.   Are you with me?''

"We sure are!'' chorused Tom and
Harry.

CHAPTER XII

BROKEN WINDOW

EARLY next morning Buddy, Tom and Harry assembled at the club house in preparation for their trip to visit the junk-dealer, Lou Farrish at Prattville. The boys were about to mount their wheels, to go and discover, if possible, the stolen red-marked sash weights, when Mr. Jonas Slarry came walking down the street.

Mr. Slarry was one of the officials of Mountchester, Buddy didn't know exactly what, but he and the other boys knew Mr. Slarry.

"Hello, boys," Mr. Slarry greeted. "I see you're off on a trip, but I wonder if you could wait long enough to do me a favor."

"Sure," said Buddy. "What is it?"

"It has to do with the salvage campaign," said Mr. Slarry.

"That's where we're going now," said Tom. "Over to Prattville."

"You can't collect scrap there and have it credited to Mountchester, boys," said the official.

"We aren't going to collect any Prattville scrap," said Harry.

"We're only going to see if we can get back some Mountchester scrap that was stolen from here."

"Well, all right," said Mr. Slarry. "Only don't get in a scrap over it."

He laughed at his own joke and Buddy and his chums joined in. After which Mr. Slarry said:

"This won't interfere with your trip. I'll tell you about it. I understand you boys have a club which is helping in the scrap drive."

"It's Buddy's Victory Club," said Tom.

"It isn't my club any more than it is of all the members," said the red-haired boy. "It's a Victory Club, all right. And if we can do anything to help, we will."

"I know you will," went on the official.
"And I think you can. I have been appointed chairman of the tin can salvage
drive and I'm having a lot of trouble."

"Do you mean the people won't turn in
their tin cans?" asked Buddy, and his voice
showed anger.

"Oh, they'll put the cans out to be collected," said Mr. Slarry, "but they won't
process them. And tin cans that aren't
processed are almost worthless for scrap.
The cans must be processed. To do that—"

"Excuse me," said Buddy, "but our club
knows all about processing cans. We
passed a resolution that every member must
see that the cans from his house are processed."

"Well, can your club help to get other
families to process their cans?" asked the
official. "That's what I came to see you
about. The mayor told me about your club.
Will you help?"

"We sure will," declared Buddy. "I'll
call a special meeting for tonight and we'll

take up this processing question. We'll get as many as possible to do it right."

"And if they won't, we will!" declared Tom.

"You said it!" added Harry.

"I might give you a few arguments as to why it is necessary to process the cans," went on Mr. Slarry. "Some questions may be asked at your meeting and you'll be able to give correct answers."

Briefly the official explained why the cans must be washed, the labels removed and the cans flattened after the tops and bottoms had been cut out. Buddy and his chums took notes and promised to explain everything at the meeting. Most of this they already knew.

"Well, that's going to be a help, I'm sure," said Mr. Slarry as the boys prepared to ride away. "I was getting worried about our tin can branch of the salvage campaign, but now I'm sure it is going to be all right."

"The Victory Club will help," promised Buddy.

It wasn't much of a bicycle ride to Prattville and the boys were soon there. They inquired the location of Lou Farrish's junk yard at a filling station. The attendant, who had just finished putting gas in a car, and collecting the ration coupon, looked sharply at Buddy and his chums as the red-haired boy made the inquiry.

"You chaps got junk to sell Farrish?" he asked.

"No," said Buddy.

"Going to buy some?" asked the man.

"Nope," answered Tom and Harry.

"Maybe you're going to work for him," suggested the attendant.

"No," said Buddy. "But if we were—"

"Well, I'd advise against it," said the man. "Some boys I know went to work for Farrish. He worked 'em hard but paid 'em poor."

"What sort of work?" asked Tom.

"Processing tin cans. This here Farrish buys a lot of junk. He gets a lot of cans

that aren't fixed right so they can be sent to
the de-tinning plants. So he hired kids to fix
the cans. But he doesn't pay 'em enough
for all their hard work. And some of the
kids get cut hands on the tins. It's hard
work.''

"No, we aren't looking for jobs," said
Buddy. "We just thought we'd look this
junk yard over. We're from Mountchester.''

"How's the scrap campaign going
there?''

"Pretty good," said Tom.

"That's fine. Well, don't trust Farrish
too far," advised the man as he went over to
service another car.

"This gives me an idea," said Buddy as
he and his chums started riding toward the
junk yard.

"In what way?" asked Harry.

"Well, I was wondering how we could get
in this junk yard without exciting suspicion,
as a detective would say. Now I know. We

can sort of pretend we're looking for work. And while we are talking to Farrish we can look around.''

"And, maybe, spot some sash weights," said Tom.

"Sure," agreed Buddy. "Let's go!"

The junk yard was rather large and was piled up with considerable scrap in the shape of iron, tin and rubber. The boys rode un-challenged into the yard, past a small shack that seemed to be an office. Out of the door came Lou Farrish. The boys recognized him as the driver of the truck on which Sid Monson and his cronies had ridden to the old stove factory.

"What you boys want?" demanded Far-rish. "You lookin' for work, maybe?"

"What kind of work?" asked Buddy. He walked over to talk to the junkman, and winked at Tom and Harry to indicate they might scout around.

"Fixing tin cans," said Farrish. "I get a lot of 'em, but they got to be fixed—

you know—cleaned and stepped on to make flat like. You boys want to do that."

"How much do you pay?" asked Buddy.

"Oh, about nine cents a hundred."

"Nine cents a hundred cans!" cried Buddy. "Why a fellow would have to process more than ten cans to earn a cent."

"It's good pay," said Kokowsky. "Take it or leave it."

"Would you make it fifteen cents a hundred?" asked Buddy, to gain time for Tom and Harry to look about. They had wandered off some distance from the shack and were peering into different junk piles.

"Fifteen cents? No, never!" cried Kokowsky. "I would be robbin' myself to do that. Hi, you! Come away from there!" he called sharply to Tom and Harry. "The tin cans aren't there."

"Oh, all right," said Tom.

"We were just looking around," spoke Harry as the two sauntered back where Buddy stood.

"I don't let no lookin' around in my yard," said the junkman. "You want to work here all right—if you don't—get out!"

"Come on," said Buddy to his chums. "We wouldn't work for that price," he added as the three rode away.

"What then you bother me for?" said the junkman angrily. "Get on out!"

"Did you see anything?" asked Buddy of his chums as they rode away.

"I saw some pieces of iron that looked like sash weights," Tom reported. "But they didn't have any red paint on."

"I didn't see them," admitted Harry. "But I sort of think this place isn't on the level."

"I think the same," said Buddy. "But I guess we can't do anything more here. We'll have to get as many as we can to the meeting tonight to have this tin can business straightened out.

"That's right," said Tom.

"It's queer people with tin cans won't do the little job of processing them to help win the war," said Harry. "I wonder if—" he ceased speaking to say in lower tones: "Look who's coming!"

It was Sid Monson, Ike Blatter and Jake Turner, in a jalopy of a car, chugging along the road in the direction of the junk yard. In the auto was a pile of iron and some rubber tires.

"Gone into the junk business?" asked Buddy as he and his chums passed Sid and the others.

"None of your business!" snapped Jake.

"If you and that fancy club of yours tries to bother us, we'll show you something!" threatened Jake.

"Go ahead!" laughed Buddy. "Show us anything you like."

"We have our eyes open," added Tom.

"And we can see sash weights in windows," called Harry as the jalopy rattled on.

"That bunch sure is teaming up with an unauthorized junkman," said Buddy as he and his chums rode on.

The meeting of the club that night was well attended. A number of new members came in and Buddy and the older members made them welcome.

"This meeting," said Buddy as the crowd of boys and girls grew as quiet as possible, "is about processing tin cans. Not enough processing is being done, and this club has got to help."

"How?" asked Wilson Smith, one of the new members.

"Well," said Buddy, "if the people who put out tin cans for the scrap collection won't take off the labels, wash the cans and flatten 'em after the tops and bottoms are out, then we'll have to do it."

"That's a lot of work," commented some one.

"Nothing is too much work for victory," said Buddy. "If anybody in the club objects, they don't have to stay in."

There was silence for a moment and Agnes Randall asked:

"Why do we have to take the paper labels off the cans?"

"This is what Mr. Slarry told me about that," said Buddy. "When the cans first come to the detinning factory, they are cleaned in big wooden vats, like a washing machine. If the paper labels are left on, they dissolve into a sort of mushy pulp and clog up the drain pipes."

"Then we certainly will wash the labels off the cans," said Agnes.

"But why do the cans have to be stepped on or flattened?" asked Lucy Gordon.

"That's because—" began Buddy. He was interrupted by a crash of glass. The window at the rear of the garage club house was broken and some object, coming through the hole, landed with a thud at Buddy's feet.

CHAPTER XIII

WARNING

SOME of the girls screamed. Some of the boys shouted. Tom and Harry, who were nearest the doors, ran out and around to the rear of the garage.

"What was it?" asked Mary Clee.

Buddy stooped to pick up the object which had been hurled at the window, breaking the glass.

"Look out!" shouted Frank Todd.

"Maybe it's a bomb!" added George Jackson.

Buddy had already picked up the object.

"It's nothing but a stone wrapped in a piece of newspaper," he said, holding up the missile. "It's wrapped in a page torn from our Mountchester paper."

Buddy took out the stone and laid it on the table near which he was standing. Then he looked at the piece of paper.

"This," he said, "is a page from the paper containing a little account of our Victory Club. It looks as if this piece of paper was used on purpose by somebody who isn't friendly to our club."

"Maybe they're jealous," suggested Agnes.

"Because we wouldn't let them join," added Lucy Gordon.

"We haven't prevented anybody from joining the club," said Buddy. "The more members we have the more scrap we can help collect. I don't know who threw this. But it didn't do much harm. A little more air in the clubhouse won't hurt. Did you see anybody?" asked Buddy of Tom and Harry who came back from their hurried trip.

"No," said Tom.

"Somebody was running away over the back lots," reported Harry. "But it was too dark to see. What did they chuck in?"

Buddy showed the stone and paper to his chum who passed it around the room.

"We'll now go on with the meeting," said the red-haired lad. "The last question was about flattening the tin cans. That's done, Mr. Slarry said, so they won't take up so much room in shipment. And a lot more flat cans can be put in the washing and de-tinning vats if the cans are flat than if they are left round. So step on all cans and tell everybody else to do the same."

"I—now—I jump on my cans with—now —both feet!" piped up little Tommie Tasker from the back of the room. Several laughed and Tommie, taking it in good part, added: "I'm not heavy enough to flatten a can with one foot."

"Then use two, Tommie," said Buddy.

More questions were asked and answered. The meeting was about to adjourn when Mr. Slarry appeared. He seemed to be in a hurry.

"I'm glad I'm in time," he said.

"Why, has anything happened?" asked Buddy.

"No. But the Council just had an emergency meeting and they passed an ordinance to make people not only process tin cans but to stop putting cans out with other garbage. From now on anybody that puts in the garbage or ashes tin cans that are needed to help win the war will be fined $10."

"Hurray!" cheered Buddy and the others joined.

"I came to tell you this," went on Mr. Slarry, "so you can pass the word to householders where you go to collect tin cans. We didn't stipulate a fine for those who won't process their cans, but we're going to get them to do it in another way."

"How?" asked Buddy.

"Like this," explained Mr. Slarry. "The mayor is going to have small warning posters printed, stating that whoever doesn't process his tin cans is hampering the war and victory effort. We'll give you club members some of these posters, and you can use them as you see fit. They are being printed tonight and I'll see that you have some in the morning, Buddy."

"Thanks! We can use them. And now, girls and fellows," went on the red-haired president. "I guess we can adjourn."

The meeting broke up. There was much talk about the new ordinance, the warning poster and the incident of the broken window.

"I'm pretty sure I know who threw the stone," said Tom.

"So am I," said Buddy. "But we can't do anything about that now. We'll have to get busy tomorrow going around telling people to do better with their tin cans."

"And what about the shack?" asked Tom.

"What shack?" Buddy asked.

"You know," added Harry. "The one out at the old stove factory. Where we saw the man run out. Don't you think we'd better take another look around there?"

"Yes," said Buddy, "I do. But we've got more important things to do first. We can go out to the shack in a couple of days. After the tin campaign is doing better."

"Maybe we'd better tell the F.B.I." suggested Tom.

"You mean about people not processing their tin cans?" asked Buddy.

"No. About the shack. It looks suspicious to me," Tom said.

"Well, we might do that," Buddy agreed.

Members of the Victory Club got busy early next morning. They started calling on the citizens asking them to make more of an effort to save and process tin cans. Nearly everyone the members appealed to were ready and anxious to cooperate.

"I never understood, until you told me," said Mrs. Watson to Tom, who visited her, "why I should take the paper off my cans. Of course I see, now, it would clog the pipes. Well, from now on I'll make my cans clean. And I'll make Mr. Watson step on 'em. He's got big feet," she added with a laugh.

Buddy found that most of those he called

on were very anxious to help. But when he knocked at the door of a house where Jabez Lent lived he was greeted by a crabbed, old man who scowled as he opened the door.

"What you want?" demanded Mr. Lent. "If you're selling anything I don't want it."

"I'm not selling anything," said Buddy. "I just want you to promise to save your tin cans, wash them, take off the labels, remove the tops and bottoms, put them inside the can and then step on it."

"What's this rigmarole?" snapped the old man. "I'll do nothing of the sort! Wash and step on tin cans! Nonsense!"

"Maybe you haven't heard," said Buddy politely, "that the government needs tin cans for victory. If you put tin cans out in your ashes and garbage, from now on, you'll be fined $10."

"Who says so?"

"The mayor and the Mountchester Council."

"Huh! I'd like to see 'em fine me $10! Nonsense!"

"And," went on Buddy, "if you don't process your cans I'll tack this notice on your house.   Maybe you'd like to read it."

Buddy handed Mr. Lent one of the posters which Mr. Slarry had, early that morning, supplied to club members and others.   It said:

THE OCCUPANT OF THIS HOUSE REFUSES TO HELP WIN THE WAR.   HE REFUSES TO PROCESS HIS TIN CANS.   ALL SCRAP IS VITAL TO THE WAR.   THIS OCCUPANT IS WORKING AGAINST VICTORY

"You mean you'll put that on my house?" shouted Mr. Lent.

"I will if you don't promise to process your cans," said Buddy firmly.

"You put that on my house and I'll rip it right off!" threatened the old man.

"Then I'll put on another," said Buddy. "I'll put this one on now.   I brought a hammer and tacks on purpose.   I didn't think

I'd need 'em, but I'm sorry to see I do."

Buddy started to tack up the notice. Mr. Lent fairly jumped out on his porch. He made a grab for Buddy, shouting:

"Don't you dare put that on my house!"

CHAPTER XIV

TWO RUN AWAY

CRABBED, old Mr. Lent was struggling with Buddy. He was trying to take away the hammer and tacks and the notice the red-haired boy was endeavoring to put on the house. A voice in the street suddenly asked:

"What's the matter, Buddy?"

Buddy saw, over his shoulder, big, good-natured, burly Policeman McGrath at the gate.

"Mr. Lent refuses to process his tin cans," said Buddy. "I'm going to put up the notice Mr. Slarry said we were to use for anybody that wouldn't help the scrap campaign."

"He isn't going to put that notice on my house!" shouted the old man.

"Maybe Buddy isn't, but I am!" said the policeman with a chuckle. "Let me have that hammer, the tacks and the notice, Buddy. I can reach up a little higher than you can.''

''Do you mean you're going to tack that— that impudent notice on my house?'' demanded the old man.

''That's what I'm going to do,'' said Policeman McGrath. ''And if you take it down I'll not only tack it up again but I'll arrest you.''

''But you can't do that to me! Nonsense!''

''Yes I can. It's legal. The Council passed emergency ordinances last night. I was at the meeting,'' said the officer holding the notice against the house and preparing to drive the first tack. ''We're in a war you know, Mr. Lent. Maybe you've forgotten.''

''Yes—yes—I sort of—forget,'' murmured the old man in calmer tones. ''I'm sorry. You needn't put that notice up. I'll do whatever is right. I'll keep my cans out of the garbage and I'll process them. I'm sorry I made trouble for you, Buddy.''

"Oh, you didn't make much trouble," grinned the red-haired boy. "I was only doing what I've been told to do."

"I realize you were. Well, I won't dispute. I'll fix my cans."

"I'm glad you came to your senses, Mr. Lent," said Policeman McGrath. "It makes it pleasanter all around. Here you are, Buddy," and he handed back the notice. "Use these at the next house where you get a refusal to process the tin cans. And if you need help, maybe I'll be passing again."

"Thank you," said Buddy. "But I guess I won't have much trouble."

He walked down the street with the officer who, nodding his head back toward Mr. Lent's house, said:

"Poor old man! He's had a lot of trouble."

"How?" asked Buddy.

"Well, he's lost nearly all his folks. He lives alone and I guess he hasn't a very happy life. He was almost rich, once, too."

"How?" asked Buddy again.

"Oh, he invented a very good patent can opener. It works fine, too. He gave me one. You fasten it on the kitchen wall, put a can in and turn a crank. It cuts the top of the can out like a wink of the eye, and leaves no rough edges. My wife thinks it's fine.

"We use it now to process all our cans, not that we have so many, but it's the quickest, handiest can opener I ever saw," said the policeman.

"If Mr. Lent got a patent on it why didn't he make some money?" asked the red-haired boy.

"Well, he got the patent, and started a company to make the can openers," said the officer. "But there was something wrong about the patent—I don't know all the details—something about an infringement. Anyhow, poor Mr. Lent lost all his money and it soured him. But he'll be all right from now on. I'll watch to see that he doesn't dump any cans in the garbage. You sort of touched him on a sore place when you asked him to process his cans, when he lost so much on a can opener," chuckled Mr. McGrath.

"I can easily guess that," said Buddy.

"But it sure is a dandy can opener," went on the officer as he left Buddy who continued on to other houses.

The red-haired boy had no further trouble that day. All the householders to whom he appealed readily agreed to process their cans and to keep them out of the garbage. One woman said:

"I'll try to do it, Buddy. But I've got a large family and I have to do all my own work. My men folks are all in defense factories, and they don't have much time to wash and flatten cans. And I'm so busy—"

Buddy had a sudden inspiration.

"Could you set the cans aside, Mrs. Burns, and let us call for them to process?"

"Why, yes, I could do that. But who would call for them?"

"Our Victory Club," said Buddy. "We

haven't done this yet, but we can. Maybe there are other women who haven't time to process their cans.''

''I don't doubt but what there are, Buddy,'' said Mrs. Burns. ''It will be fine if you can come and get my cans. I have quite a lot.''

''We'll do it,'' promised the red-haired boy. He found two or three other women like Mrs. Burns before he had finished his round of visits that day. And when Buddy went to the club meeting that night he had an enthusiastic report to make.

''Girls and boys,'' he announced, ''this club will process cans for any householders who can't do it themselves. We'll arrange to collect the opened cans, bring them here, wash off the labels, cut out the bottoms and take off the tops that are only partly cut out and then we'll—''

''Step on the cans!'' finished Tom and Harry in a duet.

''That's it, exactly!'' agreed Buddy with

a laugh. "We'll process cans right in this club, or in the garage space next door. There's water and a sink there."

"How about taking out the bottoms and taking off the tops that are partly off?" asked Ted Austin. "I cut my hand today trying to use a can opener on some of our cans." He held up a bandaged hand.

"Well," admitted Buddy, "cutting out the tops and bottoms isn't going to be easy. But we've got to do it. I guess if we wear old gloves we won't cut our hands much. It's got to be done for victory."

There was a little commotion at the rear of the room. A voice asked:

"Is this the Victory Club?"

"Yes, sir," said Agnes Randall who was near the door. "Won't you come in."

"Oh, gosh!" murmured Buddy as he saw Mr. Lent entering. "I hope he isn't going to make any more trouble."

But that was far from the old man's intention.

"I have heard, today, from Policeman McGrath," announced Mr. Lent, "that this club is helping in the war effort by collecting old tin cans for scrap. One of your members was at my house today. I'm sorry to say I wasn't as polite as I should have been, and I now beg pardon."

"That's all right, Mr. Lent," said Buddy.

"I didn't come here just for that," went on the old man. "It occurred to me that you boys—and girls—" he added with a smile, "might get a lot of cans with the bottoms and some of the tops still on. Now, a few years ago, I made a can opener that takes out tops and bottoms easily, quickly and smoothly. I want to give you a few of my openers that you can use on tin cans you collect. Good night."

He handed Agnes a small box and hurried away. For a moment no one spoke and then Agnes, opening the box, showed several of the automatic can openers.

"Say, they came in the nick of time!" exclaimed Buddy.

"Let's see how they work," suggested Frank Todd.

Directions for setting up and operating the openers were in the cartons containing them. There were screws to fasten the openers to a wall. Buddy got a screw driver from his father's auto and found a few empty cans, with the bottoms still in. When the opener was in place, and a can inserted and the crank handle turned, the can bottom was cut out cleanly and smoothly.

"This solves the problem," said Buddy.

"No more cut hands!" added Ted Austin.

"We can process all the cans in town!" declared Buddy. "Mr. Lent gave us half a dozen of his patent openers." Buddy told of his experience at Mr. Lent's house that day. Everyone agreed that the old man had more than made amends, and was truly showing the "Victory" spirit.

Next day the patent, automatic openers were set up in the club house. The girls and boys arranged to work in relays gathering the cans, washing them, taking out the tops and bottoms and then flattening the tins. In the next few days so many tin cans had accumulated at the Victory Club that Mr. Slarry sent a special city truck to pick them up for shipment to the de-tinning plant.

"Well," said Tom to Buddy and Harry the day after the collection of flat tin cans had been made, "now we have a breathing spell."

"No we haven't," said Buddy. "There's a lot more cans and other scrap to get in."

"I didn't mean we should stop," said Tom. "But can't we take a little time off to go scout around that old shack out at the stove factory?"

"I think that would be a good idea," Buddy said.

"And if we find anything suspicious, we'll tell the F.B.I." said Harry.

"Yes," agreed his red-haired chum.

Next day, having finished their scrap work, the three boys went to the old shack. They approached it quietly, but, cautious as was their approach, they were evidently discovered.

When they were a hundred feet from the lonely cabin they heard voices sounding an alarm and two men suddenly ran out of the hut, disappearing in the underbrush.

CHAPTER XV

PRISONERS

BUDDY and his chums instantly halted as the two men ran out of the lonely cabin.

"What do you make of that?" asked Tom.

"Did you ever see those men before?" Harry wanted to know.

The two chums had come, naturally in the course of their association with Buddy Martyne to let him lead. They did so now.

"I don't know what to make of it," said the red-haired boy. He ran his fingers through his already rumpled hair as if that would help him think better.

"They didn't want us to catch 'em in the shack," said Tom.

"Then they must be up to some crooked work," suggested Harry.

"Looks so," agreed Buddy. "As for ever having seen those two men before, I can't be

sure. What say we take a look inside the
shack again?"

"It might be dangerous," Tom said.

"There may be more men inside," warned
Harry.

Buddy looked carefully at the lonely
cabin. The three boys stood about a hundred feet from it. No sound was to be heard.
The place was very peaceful and quiet following the sudden rush of the two fugitives.
The sounds they had made crashing through
the woods and underbrush were no longer
noticeable.

"I don't believe there are any more men
in the cabin," Buddy said. "If the men
there were doing something they didn't want
to be caught at, they would all skip out when
we came near. Part of 'em wouldn't go and
leave others. They'd either all clear out or
all stay. They could see we are only three
boys, without even a club."

"We've got the Victory Club," ventured
Tom with a grin.

"Yes," admitted Buddy with a smile.

"And maybe the Victory Club can help solve this mystery."

"Then you think we'd better keep on and take a look inside the shack, same as we did before?" asked Tom.

"Yes," said the red-haired boy. "Let's go."

"What about each taking a club along— I mean a real club," suggested Harry. "Even if there's only one man in the shack, and he tries to hit us as we come in, we can wham him over the hand with a stick, if we each have one."

"It's a good idea," Buddy admitted. "Get sticks."

The boys soon armed themselves with stout cudgels and then, as cautiously as before, advanced on the cabin. Silence still shrouded it. The mystery appeared to deepen.

Step by step, now and then pausing to listen and observe, Buddy, Tom and Harry drew nearer and nearer the lonely shack. Now and then they glanced up at the old stove factory below which the shack was built. The factory seemed as deserted and silent as was the little cabin from which two men had run away.

Suddenly Buddy stooped, picked up a stone and hurled it at the shack. It struck the front with an echoing thud.

"What'd you do that for?" asked Tom in a whisper.

"Just to see what would happen," Buddy explained. "If there's anybody still in the cabin, sort of hiding away so they can't see us, that stone will give 'em notice we're still on the job."

"Not a bad idea," commented Harry.

But the trial shot brought no response or signal from the cabin. It remained as silent as before. There was no sign of life.

"Let's go!" said Buddy in a tense whisper, after a moment or two of anxious waiting. He led the way. Tom and Harry followed, side by side, their clubs held in readiness.

They reached the entrance to the cabin

without being challenged. They entered without anyone opposing them. A glance around the interior of the small shack showed it to be unoccupied. But the same glance showed a few articles on the make-shift bench that had not been there before. The alarm clock was still ticking away. It was on the bench and near it were some sheets of paper and the stub of a pencil.

Buddy quickly looked at the sheets. There was nothing on the paper. But some of the sheets bore faint impressions as if sheets on top of them had been used to write on and then taken away.

"Say, maybe this is some place where an artist comes to make sketches for pictures," said Tom as he looked at the pencil.

"Or maybe," ventured Harry, "somebody is writing a book here. Fellows that write books do funny things. They like to go off in the woods to be quiet and by themselves."

"That's right," Buddy agreed. "But if the men here were just artists or authors they wouldn't run away as scared as these two men seemed to be. There's nothing wrong about making pictures or writing books.''

''Unless the men are spies and are making sketches of our national defense and war effort,'' said Tom.

''Golly! That may be it!'' exclaimed Harry.

''What is there around here that has to do with war or defense?'' asked Buddy. He motioned to the quiet stream and the lonely, deserted glen through which it flowed. ''Spies wouldn't have any object in hiding away in this shack. There's no defense plant around here.''

''There is at Prattville,'' said Tom.

''That's right,'' added Harry. ''There's a lot of factories there that make shell casings and airplane parts.''

''Prattville is quite a distance from here,'' said Buddy.

''But the spies could go there and meet

here to draw out their plans and make up reports,'' insisted Harry.

"I don't believe this will turn out to be anything like that,'' said Buddy. "These men are probably tramps. This is one of their hangouts or hideouts. Look, there's another bag that's had food in it.'' He picked the bag from the floor. It was greasy and had crumbs still remaining in it.''

"The two men who ran out sure did look like tramps,'' admitted Tom.

"And they both needed shaves,'' added Harry. "Tramps almost always do. They don't get time to shave.''

"Well, this looks as if one of them intended to shave,'' said Buddy suddenly. He stooped to the floor of the cabin and, near where he had found the paper food bag, picked up a safety razor. "I guess we interrupted the barber,'' said Buddy.

He was still bending over, from having stooped to pick up the razor, when he suddenly began tossing aside a litter of paper and leaves on the floor.

"See anything else?" asked Tom.

"Look," said Buddy, pointing.

"Wires!" exclaimed Harry. "There are insulated wires under the leaves."

"And they run up toward the old stove factory," said Buddy as he tossed aside more litter on the floor. "Fellows, we've found something. Let's trace these wires!"

The boys did this. They found that the insulated wires extended outside the shack, in a shallow trench in the ground, covered with leaves, sticks and dirt. The wires ran to the side of the slope, atop of which was built the old factory. There the wires entered a two inch iron pipe that had evidently been used as a water drain. This discovery had now aroused their curiosity.

"The wires go in the factory!" said Buddy, now greatly excited. "We'll go in and see where they end."

The three boys scrambled up the embankment and were soon in the old factory. They paused to look and listen but neither saw nor heard anything suspicious.

"Where do the wires come out in here?" asked Tom.

"That's what we've got to discover," Buddy said. "Scout around, fellows!"

The three separated and went into various rooms of the old factory. They found no place where the wires emerged. But Tom, who had gone down a rickety flight of steps, suddenly called:

"Fellows, I've found something!"

"What?" asked Buddy.

"It looks like a secret room. Come on down."

Harry and Buddy climbed down the rickety stairs leading to the lower floor of the old factory.

"Gosh! It's dark here," said Harry.

"Mind your step," warned Tom. "I wish I'd brought my flashlight."

"I did," said Buddy. "I just remembered I have a small one."

"Then flash it!" said Harry. "I can't see a thing."

Soon a little gleam of light illuminated the darkness of the factory cellar.

"I don't see how you found this without a light, Tom," said Buddy.

"It isn't so dark after your eyes get used to it. You couldn't see because you just came down. If you wait about half a minute you can see fairly well without the flash light. But it's just what we need. Let's take a look in this secret room."

Buddy and Harry found that Tom had spoken correctly. It was now less dark in the cellar and the room, partitioned off in one corner, was fairly visible.

Once more Buddy took the lead, with his light. He went in the room. Tom and Harry followed. Buddy was flashing his little electric torch around the walls of the room. There were some chairs and a table in the place; nothing else as far as the boys at first noticed.

But they suddenly became aware of foot-steps approaching down the steps and along

the dark cellar toward the secret room.
"Who's there?" challenged Buddy.

There was no answer. But, a moment
later, the door was slammed shut and the
boys heard a heavy bar dropped into place,
outside it.

They were prisoners.

CHAPTER XVI

THREE GIRLS

FOR a moment Buddy and his chums did not exactly know what had happened. True, they had heard footsteps coming and going. They had heard the thud as the heavy bar, outside the door, was pushed into the side braces. Momentarily they wished they had noticed that the door could be barred from the outside. But it was too late, now.

Tom, who was nearest the door, turned and began pushing on it as hard as he could. It was a heavy door, he noted, and it held firmly.

"Hey, let us out of here!" yelled Tom, pounding with his fists.

"Who did it?" asked Harry. "Is it a joke?"

"This door is no joke!" exclaimed Tom.

155

"Swing your light around this way, Buddy."

The red-haired boy flashed the gleam of his little torch on the door. It fitted closely into the frame. There was neither knob nor latch on the inside of the portal.

"Bring the light a little closer," begged Tom. "Maybe there's a crack or an opening we can get our hands in and pull the door open."

"The door shuts inward," said Buddy. "Pulling wouldn't do any good. We'll have to push."

"Well, then, help me push!" panted Tom, who changed his tactics from pounding with his fists to pushing. "Show more light, Buddy. I don't know which side the hinges are on."

"No hinges show from inside," said Buddy as he focused the gleam of his small electric torch all around the edges of the door. "And I don't want to keep my light on too long. The batteries aren't fresh. If they give out on us we'll be in the dark."

"Gosh! It is dark in here!" said Harry when Buddy, as a conservation measure, shut off his light for a moment.

"Anybody got any matches?" asked Buddy as he turned on the gleam again.

"I have," Harry said. "But we haven't any candles and you can't use matches in a flash light."

"No," said Buddy. "A match, though, will light a sliver of wood and we can use that for a torch. I see some pieces of wood on the floor. Pick 'em up. They'll help when my flash light gives out."

Tom and Harry scrambled to pick up some sticks from the floor of the inner, secret room of the old stove factory. What it had been used for the boys did not know. It was about ten feet square and almost as high. It was covered smoothly with matched boards on the inside.

"Looks as if it might have been used as an ice box or refrigerator," commented Buddy as he flashed his light on and off to make observations.

"What would they want with an ice box in a stove factory?" asked Harry. "To keep the grates from getting overheated?"

"They might have stored chemicals here," said Buddy. "They use chemicals in making iron castings and maybe some kinds may have to be kept cool."

"It does look like an old ice box," agreed Tom. "The door seems heavy and double thick. And ice box doors don't have knobs or handles on the inside."

"Well, whoever fastened us in here must know we can't get out easily," said Harry. There was a note of anxiety in his voice. "I wonder how we're going to get out?"

"It isn't going to be easy," Buddy said. "Have you fellows got knives?" He produced his own, a Boy Scout knife. Tom and Harry carried knives like Buddy's.

"Good!" exclaimed the red-haired lad. "Maybe we can cut a hole through the door and lift up the bar. If we can do that we'll

get out. But it isn't going to be easy to
make a hole in this door. It's good and
solid!" He proved this by jabbing his knife
blade in several places. "But I guess it's
the only way," Buddy added as he flashed
his light around the room again. "Let's
start. But we'll work by torches and not by
my flashlight. I've got to save the batteries.
Where are those matches, Harry?"

"Here you are!"

Buddy lighted a stick and stuck it upright in a crack in the floor the boards of
which were wider and less tightly fitted than
the sides. The blazing stick gave a little
more general illumination than had the
flashlight. The boys could see they were
shut up in a tight, windowless room, the
only door securely barred from outside.

"Regular prison," commented Tom.

"I wonder who shut us up in here?"
asked Harry.

"Maybe those two men we surprised,"
said Buddy. "Or maybe Sid Monson and
his gang. They have it in for us because I

think they have guessed we suspect them of
stealing sash weights."

"But how did Sid and his crowd know we
were coming here?" asked Tom.

"They couldn't exactly know it," Buddy
said. "But they may have been scouting
around the old factory for scrap iron we
missed locating. They could have seen us
come in, and, maybe they watched us go
down here. It would be easy enough for
them to sneak up and lock us in."

"You're right, Buddy," agreed Harry.
"Or, of course, those two men could have
come back. I wonder if it would do any
good to yell?" he asked.

"What for?" inquired Tom.

"So somebody would hear and let us out."

"It isn't very likely anybody would be
around here," said Buddy, "but the persons
who locked us in. And they won't let us
out."

"Do you think they mean to—to keep us
in here until—until we—" Harry did not

finish his question but his chums knew what he had in mind.

"They'll keep us in here as long as they can," said Buddy. "Maybe after they think they have scared us off their trail they may sneak back, after dark, and let us out. But we won't wait for that. We'll start cutting our way out. We'll cut a hole about here," and he indicated the center of the door. "Then we can reach out and raise the bar. We'll take turns with our knives. There won't be room for all three of us to work side by side. We won't need a very big hole to reach out and yank up the bar. I'll start."

"Let's give a couple of shouts first," suggested Harry.

"All right. All together now!" said Buddy.

The boys shouted vigorously. But though the echoes of their voices sounded deafeningly in their own ears, it was doubtful if their call carried far outside.

Then Buddy began to cut. He was skillful with his knife and soon had outlined a hole about six inches square and began cutting out slivers of wood from each side.

"Fellows, don't you think it's getting sort of stuffy and smoky in here?" asked Tom a few minutes later as Buddy stopped to rest.

"It is close," agreed Harry. "I—I guess this place is almost airtight. It would need to be if it was a refrigerator. I—I feel kind of queer. I'm going to lie down."

Harry didn't exactly stretch himself out easily. He toppled to the floor. Buddy stopped cutting and whipped out his flashlight. He focused it on Harry's face.

"The air—the air's getting bad in here," murmured Tom. "I guess you'd better put out that blazing stick, Buddy. It's burning up all the oxy—the oxy—"

Buddy kicked over and stepped on the blazing stick. Then he, too, felt dizzy and faint.

"There's fresher air near the floor," he said. "You fellows keep lying down. I'll

join you. Don't worry! We'll get out of
here."

"We've got to—pretty soon—or
smother," murmured Tom.

Buddy's heart was pounding hard. He
and his chums were in a tough spot and they
knew it. The Victory Club seemed very far
away, now.

But in the room of the Victory Club, at
that moment, three girls were putting up
fresh curtains, having washed the original
set.

"I wonder where the boys are?" said
Agnes Randall. "None of them has been
around all day."

"Maybe they're out getting more scrap,"
suggested Lucy Gordon.

"I heard Harry say they were going to
the old stove factory," said Mary Clee. "He
and Tom and Buddy started for there."

"Let's go look for them," said Agnes.
"Here's a letter the postman just left. It's
for the Victory Club. Maybe Buddy might

want it.   Let's go out to the old factory, now we have the curtains hung.''

"Maybe the boys wouldn't like us following them," said Mary.

"They can't object.   We're all members of the club," said Agnes.   "Come on, let's go!"

After a little further argument, the three girls started for the old stove factory.

CHAPTER XVII

JUST IN TIME

BUDDY and his imprisoned chums found the air much fresher and better to breathe when they either fell, or plumped, to the floor of the old ice box. Tom and Harry soon revived. Buddy, who had also begun to feel faint and ill as the air grew more impure, recovered more rapidly. He was the more robust of the three.

"What happened?" murmured Tom as he started to sit up.

"Keep lying down!" warned Buddy.

"We must have burned up a lot of the oxygen in this place," said Harry.

"We did," admitted Buddy. "I didn't think that the blazing wood was going to do that. But we're all right now."

"For how long," asked Tom, dubiously.

"For as long as we keep near the floor," said Buddy.

"Then can't we stand up and hack away at the hole in the door?" asked Harry.

Buddy thought this over for a moment before he answered. He rose to his knees and sniffed the air. It seemed fairly good.

"I have an idea," he said. "I'll try an experiment and then you fellows can do the same. Let me get close to the door."

"Are you going to stand up and use your knife again?" asked Tom.

"Don't," advised Harry. "The bad air rises, as it's lighter than regular air. The higher you are the worse the air is. I guess we'd pass out cold if we were near the ceiling."

"I know," said Buddy. "I'm not going to stand up yet. But if I can prove what I think I can, we'll soon be able to stand." He moved over close to the bottom of the door and put his nose to the crack, if it could be called a crack, where the door fitted into the lower edge of the frame. The door fitted so tightly elsewhere that there was hardly a wide enough crack for Buddy to put his knife blade in.

Buddy began to breathe in deeply.

"What's the matter?" asked Tom, anxiously.

"You going to pass out again?" asked Harry.

"No," the red haired boy answered. "But I'm right. There's some fresh air coming in through this bottom crack—not much, but some. You fellows take sniffs."

Tom and Harry put their noses to the bottom crack and breathed in deeply.

"You're right," said Tom.

"It's fresh air, and it smells fine!" exclaimed Harry. "But we can't keep lying here on the floor, just to breathe. It isn't very comfortable."

"We won't have to lie here very long," Buddy said. "The fresh air will gradually displace the foul air we breathed, which made us sick and faint. It may take a little while, but it's sure. There must be some ventilation to this place—more than I thought at first.''

"But we won't be able to burn the wood for light, will we?'' asked Tom.

"No, we won't dare risk that,'' Buddy said. "The flame burns up the oxygen too fast. We'll have to use my flash light to see to dig a hole in the door. I don't know how long the batteries will last but we'll have to chance it. We don't want to stay here all night.''

"How long do you think we've been in here now?'' asked Tom.

"Well,'' calculated Buddy, "it was about 10 o'clock when we got here. What with watching those men and exploring the old factory and getting in here, I guess we spent more than three hours.''

"Then it's after noon—past lunch time!'' exclaimed Tom.

"Yes,'' said Buddy, "it is.''

"My stomach says so, anyhow,'' commented Harry. "I'm hungry. How about standing up now, Buddy.''

"I guess we can take a chance. But wait until I try it."

The red-haired boy rose cautiously to his feet, sniffing the air several times during his progress. When he was standing upright he took a long breath and said:

"It's all right. Stand up."

"And start digging!" cried Harry. "It's my turn."

"And I'll take a turn after you," offered Tom.

"Here's the light," said Buddy, switching on his little torch. "I'll hold it for you."

In the gleam of the little torch, which, the boys could see, was slowly getting dimmer as the batteries became exhausted, Tom vigorously attacked the tough wood of the door. He dug in the slight depression Buddy had made.

Suddenly Tom uttered an exclamation of dismay.

"What's the matter?" asked Buddy. "Cut yourself?"

"No, but I snapped off my knife blade."

It fell to the floor with a metallic clang.

"Too bad," said the red-haired boy.
"Take yours, Harry, and go slow. We'll
have to depend on our two knives, now, for
getting out of here."

"I'm sorry," said Tom. "I went at it too
fast."

"Never mind," consoled Buddy. "I guess
we can manage with my knife and Harry's.
But go slow," he warned Harry who was
opening his knife. And don't cut yourself."

Harry was a more skillful whittler than
was Tom, and really made the chips and
splinters fly. But at that it was slow work.
His arm and wrist soon began to ache and
pain.

"I wish I could use my left hand," he said.
"I wonder if I could shift over."

"Better not try it," said Buddy. "You
may break your knife. It's my turn now,
anyhow. Here, Tom, you hold the light."

"Anyhow, I can dig with Harry's knife
when you get tired," Tom said. "That will
let Harry's arm rest."

So, by turns, the boys hacked and whittled away at the door. Every now and then they would stop and look at the progress they had made in the glow of Buddy's torch.

"What say we give another shout?" asked Tom after a while. "We aren't cutting through that door very fast."

"No," admitted Buddy. "It's slow work. But I don't see what good shouting will do. Nobody ever comes here—or hardly ever."

"I'm going to yell, anyhow," declared Tom. "You fellows can join in. It will be a change from digging."

The three yelled vigorously, calling:

"Help! Help! Help!"

It was the simplest signal they could sound. They waited and called again, several times. But there was no answer.

"We'd better start digging again," said Buddy. "I'll switch on the light." The flash light had been shut off as they shouted.

"It's my turn to dig," Harry said. "Show a light, Buddy."

Buddy did not answer for a moment.

"Show a light," said Harry.

"I can't," replied Buddy in a low voice. "The batteries are dead."

For a moment no one spoke. Then Harry asked in a low voice:

"What are we going to do?"

"I'm going to yell again!" cried Tom. "I thought I heard a noise up in the factory. Somebody may be there. Yell for all you're worth, fellows! Yell your heads off!"

They shouted again:

"Help! Help! Help!"

A moment of silence and then, faint and far off, a girl's voice asked:

"Who are you? Where are you? What's the matter?"

CHAPTER XVIII

F.B.I.

THE joyful reaction on the part of Buddy and his friends was so great, after hearing the girl's voice, that, for a moment, not one of the young prisoners could say a word. Then Buddy exclaimed:

"That's my cousin Agnes!"

"She came to find us! Fine girl!" said Tom.

"I don't see how she knew we were here," added Harry.

"It's probably just an accident that she came here," said Buddy. "But it's a lucky accident for us," he added. Then in a burst of joy he jumped up in the dark room and clicked his heels together three times, as his uncle had taught him.

A moment later another girl's voice called:

"Is that you, Tom?"

"That's my sister Lucy," said young Mr. Gordon happily.

And then three girlish voices called in chorus:

"Where are you?"

"I'm here!" answered Tom. "We're all here. Come and let us out. We're locked in."

"I heard Mary's voice," announced Harry Clee.

"It's our three girl members," announced Buddy. "It doesn't matter how they got here as long as they're here. Come down the cellar steps!" he shouted as a direction. "Over in the northwest corner on the first floor," he added as a sort of Boy Scout, compass direction.

"But be careful coming down the stairs," added Tom.

"If you come down a few steps and then close your eyes and wait, you can see better in the dark," said Harry.

"Like when you first go in the movies to an afternoon show," directed Buddy, thinking this would be the most practical illustration he could suggest.

"We're coming!" announced Agnes.

"How ever did you get locked in down there?" asked Lucy.

"Never mind that part," the boys heard Mary Clee say. "Let's get 'em out and they can tell us afterward."

"Wise girl, Mary!" complimented her brother. "We can't get out any too soon. Mind your step!"

"I will!" Mary said.

A little later, cautious feet could be heard descending the stairs. Then there was silence.

"They're shutting their eyes and waiting until they can see better," said Buddy.

He was right for, a little later, the feet were again heard descending the steps.

"Which way do we go now?" asked Agnes. It was evident the three girls were in a huddle at the foot of the stairs in the dark cellar.

"Can you see anything?" asked Buddy.

"Not very much," Lucy answered. "It's awful dark."

"I hope there are no rats—or mice!" exclaimed Mary.

"Oh-ee-ee-ee!" screamed Agnes. "Don't talk like that!"

"There isn't even a baby mouse," declared Tom. "It's perfectly safe. Come on and raise the bar."

"What bar?" asked his sister.

"Listen!" called Buddy. "Walk toward the sound of our voices. We will keep on talking as soon as I tell you what to do. You'll see a sort of room, maybe an old, big ice box partitioned off in one corner of the cellar. The door is shut and held in place by a wooden or iron bar across it. The bar fits into pieces of iron on each side, shaped like the letter L turned on its side. Just raise the bar and we can push open the door and get out easily enough."

"Are you all right?" asked Lucy.

"Yes, but we had a tough time," said Tom.

"Why did you shut yourselves up in there?" asked Agnes.

"Never mind that now. Please let us out. Walk toward our voices and you'll see the barred door," directed Buddy. "Has any one of you got a flashlight?"

"No," answered Agnes, for all three.

"Well, maybe you can make out the place," Buddy went on.

"Oh, I see it!" cried Mary. "It's over in that corner! Come on!"

The three girls hastened in the right direction, guided by the voices of the boys who shouted loudly.

"I hope whoever dropped that bar in place didn't lock it," said Tom as he paused for breath.

"If it's locked, we're out of luck," added Harry.

"Well, if it's locked, the girls can go for help, now they know where we are," said Buddy.

The bar was not fastened in place, and,

after a few pushes and shoves, the girls were able to raise it. Then, with joyful shouts, the boys pushed the door open from inside and stepped out of their prison. It was too dark for either party to see the relieved looks on the faces of the other. But they were all happy over the successful outcome of the misadventure.

"What happened?" asked Agnes.

"Tell you when we get up where it's light," said Buddy. "Come on, I'm as dry as a fish!"

"There's a spring back of the old factory," said Mary.

"We got drinks there just before we came in to look around," added Lucy.

"Did you come here to look for us?" asked Buddy as he led the way up the stairs into the old factory.

"Sort of," admitted Agnes. "We heard you say you were coming here. I thought maybe to look for more scrap. So we thought maybe we could help. And I brought this letter."

"Oh, yes," said Buddy, reading it. "Just a note from Mrs. Knox, asking us to call to get some tin cans she has been saving. We'll get them tomorrow."

"We came here right after putting up new curtains in the Victory Club," said Lucy. "You boys work so hard getting in the scrap."

"Fine work!" commended Buddy. "But we didn't come here exactly to look for scrap. I guess this place is about cleaned out. But we came here to find out something."

"What?" asked the three girls in a chorus, scenting a secret. "You must tell us; after all we're club members, too."

"Tell you after I get a drink," promised Buddy.

Then, when he and his chums had drunk and had washed off some of the dirt and grime encountered in their stay in the old ice box, they related what had happened. They told of the two men running away from the shack, of the discovery of the wires lead-

ing into the factory and of their entrance
into the secret room, or old ice box.

"But who shut the door, dropped the bar
and locked you in—that is not exactly
locked, but kept you there?" asked Agnes.

"We don't know," Tom said.

"But we're going to find out!" asserted
Harry.

"And we're going to get the F.B.I. to help
us!" exclaimed Buddy.

"What? The 'G' men?" exclaimed Tom.

"That's right," Buddy went on. "I think
there's more going on around here than just
Sid Monson and his gang trying to sneak
away with scrap, or steal sash weights," said
the red-haired boy. "This lonely shack, the
men running away and the wires—I think
maybe it's spies or saboteurs."

"Of course then you ought to tell the
Federal Bureau of Investigation!" declared
Agnes.

"That's just what we're going to do,"
Buddy said. "On to the F.B.I., fellows!"

"Do they have any here in Mountchester?" asked Tom.

"Mayor Doremus will know," said Buddy. "We'll go see him."

"It's pretty late to go now," said Harry. "It's almost supper time," he added, looking at the declining sun. "I'm hungry."

"So am I," said Buddy. "So are a lot of our soldiers and sailors, maybe. They don't wait for supper to fight. And we aren't going to wait until after supper to tell the F.B.I. this place ought to be investigated."

"That's right!" exclaimed Agnes with enthusiasm. "I think you ought to tell the police before you eat." The others shared this feeling and Harry, seeing he was outvoted said, "Oh, I'm not so hungry but what I can wait. But maybe we ought to tell our folks about this first."

"Yes," said Buddy, "I suppose we ought. Mayor Doremus will probably be out of his office now and we'll have to go to his house.

It's quite a ways out. Tell you what, Agnes. You and Mary and Lucy go to my house and tell my mother and ask her to tell Mrs. Gordon and Mrs. Clee. Then if my father is home, and I think he will be by this time, ask him to come out here in the auto and get us and take us to the F.B.I.''

"Has he got any gas?" asked Tom.

"He can get it for a job like this!" declared Buddy. "Go on, girls. We'll stick here until my father comes for us. Maybe those men might come back," he added in lower tones to his chums.

"Oh, won't that be dangerous?" asked Mary.

"No, it won't!" decided Buddy. "You won't be long. We'll wait here and see what happens."

CHAPTER XIX

THE RAID

THOUGH they were tired, hungry and exhausted from their imprisonment, Buddy and his chums, resting only briefly after the girls had gone, made another search in and around the old factory.

They also went down to the lonely shack but discovered nothing more than they had seen at first. There was no sign that the two men, who had fled so hastily on the arrival of the boys, had returned. The uncovered wires were just as Buddy had left them after locating them.

"I'd like to know where these wires run and what they're for," said Tom.

"I'd like to know who locked us in that ice box," exclaimed Harry.

"I think we'll have answers to both questions as soon as the F.B.I. gets busy on this case," said Buddy.

"Do you really think it is a case for the G men?" asked Tom.

"I'm sure it is!" declared the red-haired boy.

The sun was sinking behind the hills to the west of Patton Creek when Buddy heard his father hailing him. The boys were still down in the glen where stood the lonely shack.

"Coming, Dad!" Buddy answered. He and his chums scrambled up the embankment to see Mr. Martyne waiting out in the road in his auto. The girls were not with him, but it was evident they had delivered Buddy's message.

"Well, your Victory Club seems to be going places, Buddy!" said Mr. Martyne with a laugh.

"Oh, yes," agreed the red-haired boy. "Did the girls tell you what happened?"

"Most of it, I guess. It was a lucky thought of theirs to go to this old factory after you. Maybe you boys shouldn't take such chances."

"You've got to take chances in war," said Buddy. "Now, dad, we want to get to the mayor's office or his house as fast as we can to have him start the F.B.I. on this case."

"I think I'd better take you to Chief of Police Burke," said Mr. Martyne. "I made some inquiries after the girls talked to me and before I started out here. Chief Burke knows how to get in touch with the 'G' men."

"Are there any around here?" asked Tom.

"Yes," said Mr. Martyne. "The chief tells me they have been here some time working on a spy case. Whether it's this one you boys may have stumbled on I don't know. But you'll soon find out."

"G men around here!" exclaimed Tom, in somewhat awed tones.

"They must have been keeping under cover," said Harry.

"That's how the F.B.I. does its best work," said Buddy. "You never know a G man when you see him. He might be sitting next to you in the movies or be taking an ice cream soda at the same counter with you. You never know.''

''Do you think the G men will consider that what we have to tell them amounts to anything?'' asked Buddy of his father as the little party started back to town.

''Well, yes, I think they will,'' said Mr. Martyne. ''Whether it's a small case or a big case I don't know. The F.B.I. isn't much given to talk until the case is closed.''

''Where will we find the G men?'' asked Buddy as they neared the main street of Mountchester. ''I didn't know they had a headquarters here.''

''They haven't,'' said Mr. Martyne. ''But after I heard the girls' story and talked to Chief Burke, he promised to have some of the G men in his office. We're going to meet them there.''

''Good!'' exclaimed Buddy.

''Gosh!'' exclaimed Tom. ''I never met a G man.''

''Neither did I,'' added Harry.

"I guess they look just like other men," remarked Buddy. "We'll soon find out."

"What's the matter, Harry?" asked Tom, noting that his chum seemed to hesitate. "Don't you want to come?"

"Oh, yes, sure. But I was thinking—"

"You were thinking of something to eat, weren't you?" asked Buddy.

"Well, sort of," admitted Harry.

"Haven't you boys had anything to eat?" asked Mr. Martyne, looking at his watch.

"Not since breakfast," answered Buddy.

"Then before we have a talk with the F.B.I. men, you boys are going to eat," said his father. "Come with me."

He took them to a lunch wagon, as being the nearest and quickest place, and the boys proved they had good appetites. Feeling better, they rode with Mr. Martyne to town.

Chief Burke welcomed the boys and Mr. Martyne in his private office. He knew Buddy and his chums for the three, with other boys in Mountville, were members of the School Patrol and the chief often spoke at their meetings.

"What's this I hear about you?" chuckled the chief. "Getting ready to team up with the G men?"

"Not quite yet," said Buddy. "And I don't know," he added modestly, "that what we saw and found out will be worth investigation by the F.B.I."

"We'll let them judge that," said the chief. "Suppose you tell me all about it first."

Which Buddy did, with some assistance from his chums when he forgot or omitted certain details.

"Um," mused Chief Burke. "Sounds very suspicious to me—especially those wires and the old ice box in the cellar."

"We'd like to find out who shut us in there," said Tom.

"If it was Sid Monson and his gang," said Harry, "we can settle with them ourselves, Chief."

"I don't believe it was that gang," said Chief Burke with a smile. "But perhaps it was. The F.B.I. may know. Better ask them. Now about these paint-daubed sash weights and that Farrish junkman at Prattville. Tell me more about him."

This the boys did. And when Buddy was speaking he suddenly interrupted himself to look at an open doorway in the rear of the chief's office and exclaim:

"There they are now!"

"Who?" asked the chief, not turning to look.

"The two men who ran out of the shack!" cried Buddy jumping to his feet.

"The same ones!" added Tom and Harry.

"Take it easy," laughed the chief. "Come on in, Mr. Godfrey and Mr. Trainter," he added. "You are discovered."

"But we can't take off our whiskers and disguises, as we will still need them," said the taller of the two men who was introduced as Mr. Godfrey.

"I think we can make the raid tonight, chief," said Mr. Trainter.

"Raid!" exclaimed Tom.

"Tonight?" echoed Harry.

"Say, are you G men?" burst out Buddy in some confusion.

"Yes, we are members of the Federal Bureau of Investigation," said Mr. Godfrey. "Here's my identification card," and he showed an official one with his photograph.

"Though the picture doesn't look as I look now," he added.

"And I am much better looking than in this rig, as you can see," added Mr. Trainter with a laugh as he showed the boys his government identification card.

"And are you the two who were in the shack?" asked Buddy.

"Yes," said Mr. Godfrey.

"And you ran away when we came along," added Tom.

"Yes. We didn't want to be discovered

just yet, even by you boys, though we knew you were all right," said Mr. Trainter. "So we beat it, as the case wasn't yet ready for the raiding stage. It is now."

"Were you in that shack the other time?" asked Buddy.

"You mean when you surprised a man you took to be a tramp and he ran out?" asked Mr. Godfrey.

"Yes," assented the red-haired lad.

"That was one of our men," said Mr. Godfrey. "He laid the ground work for what is going to happen tonight. He's in the offing now."

"But he'll be with us tonight," said Mr. Trainter.

"Could you tell us now, what those wires were for?" asked Buddy.

"Well, there's no harm telling you boys now, though the whole story won't be released until tomorrow," spoke Mr. Godfrey. "After we cage the birds it will all come out."

"If the birds come in," suggested Mr. Trainter.

"Oh, they'll come. They're all set to pull something at that defense plant at Prattville," said Mr. Godfrey.

"Then they really are spies?" asked Tom. The two F.B.I. men nodded.

"And saboteurs?" asked Harry.

"A mixture of both," said Mr. Godfrey. "We learned that by listening over a dictaphone. One end of the dictaphone was in the shack and the other end in the old ice box, where the spies met."

"Then that's what the wires were for!" exclaimed Buddy.

"Exactly," said Mr. Godfrey. "We're glad you boys didn't broadcast such discoveries as you made, or our game might have been spoiled. You did as good a job on that as your club has done in the tin can and scrap drive, which the chief tells me you are active in. Good work. And now—"

The chief's telephone rang.

"It's for you," the chief said after listening a moment. He handed the receiver to Mr. Godfrey. And the G man, after listening briefly, looked up at his companion and said:

"It's all settled. We pull the raid at midnight!"

CHAPTER XX

OVER THE TOP

THE two G men made ready to leave.

"Thanks for your help, Chief," said Mr. Godfrey to the Mountchester police head.

"We may be seeing you again," added Mr. Trainter. "The cleaning out of this nest of spies doesn't mean we have them all."

"Will you need any help from my men to help capture the gang?" asked the chief.

"We may," said Mr. Godfrey. "It wouldn't be a bad idea to have a few reserves in readiness. But a pretty big squad of our own men is on the way here. They'll give us all the help we'll need, I think. However, you never can tell what's going to happen. Thanks for your offer, and please hold some of your men subject to call."

"I'll do that," promised Chief Burke.

"And thanks to you boys, and you, also, Mr. Martyne," said Mr. Trainter. "You boys nearly spilled the beans for us, prowling around the shack we fixed up for a listening post," he went on. "That's why we sort of gave it the look of a tramps' hangout. And that's why we skipped out when you sneaked up on us."

"You put on a pretty good tramp act yourselves," complimented Chief Burke. "You sure look the parts."

"And I feel them," chuckled Mr. Godfrey. "I'll be glad to get a bath and into clean clothes. But we had to adopt these disguises to fool the gang of spies."

"Have you got good evidence against them?" asked Buddy.

"Yes, quite conclusive," said Mr. Trainter. "They held several meetings in the old ice box. We listened to their talk over our dictaphone and made notes."

"We saw some of the notes," said Tom.

"You did?" exclaimed the G men.

"Well, just impressions on some blank

paper you left in the shack," explained Harry. "We couldn't read the notes. We left them there."

"No, I guess you couldn't read them," said Mr. Godfrey. "They were in code. But it's as well you didn't disturb anything. Much obliged to you boys. And now we'll say goodbye."

Buddy had a sudden inspiration.

"Could we watch the raid?" he asked. "I mean from a distance so we wouldn't be in the way. We'd like to see what happens."

"That would be swell!" exclaimed Harry.

"Count me in," added Tom.

The two F.B.I. men exchanged glances and then looked at Mr. Martyne.

"What do you say, Godfrey?" asked Mr. Trainter.

"It's all right with me. The boys deserve a little reward for what they have done— the tin cans, scrap and everything. If you say it's all right with you, Mr. Martyne, the boys could watch—say from the road in front of the old factory."

"I'll take them there if you think there won't be any shooting," said Buddy's father.

"No, there won't be any of that. We'll jump the gang so fast they won't have time to draw their guns. Anyhow, we expect to corral them in the old ice box," said Mr. Godfrey.

"We'll make 'em come out, one at a time, with their hands in the air," said Mr. Trainter. "So it will be safe."

"Oh, thanks a lot!" exclaimed Buddy.

"You can't exactly have ring-side seats," stipulated Mr. Godfrey. "And you'll have to remain very quiet, in a place I'll post you, and not get there ahead of time. I'll fix the hour."

"We'll do just as you say!" promised the red-haired boy.

"Sure!" echoed Tom and Harry.

Then Buddy, in his joy, leaped up into the air in the chief's office and clapped his heels together three times.

"Say, that's quite a trick!" complimented

Mr. Godfrey as he and his partner laughed.

"My uncle taught it to me," said Buddy.

"You can do it again, after we capture the gang," said Mr. Trainter. "Well, let's get going," he added.

"Yes," assented Mr. Godfrey. "There's a lot to do yet."

"Do you think," asked Buddy when the time and place for the observation of the raid had been fixed, "that Sid Monson and his gang locked us in that ice box?"

"I think very likely it was," said Mr. Godfrey. "None of the gang of spies was in this neighborhood the time you say you were locked in. I think it must have been your friends who played that trick on you."

"They're no friends of ours!" declared Buddy.

"And the next time we see 'em, we'll knock 'em down and drag 'em out!" threatened Harry.

"We might have been shut in that ice box a week, if it hadn't been for the girls," said Tom.

"Oh, one of our men would have been investigating around the old factory inside that time," said Mr. Godfrey. "They would have heard your shouts. But the girls did a good job."

"They belong to our Victory Club," said Buddy, proudly.

"Some club!" commented Chief Burke. "Drop in and see me any time you need help, boys," he added to Buddy and his chums as they left the office. The G men also departed. Everything was in readiness for the midnight raid.

"Isn't it swell we can watch it!" exclaimed Buddy as he and his chums rode away with Mr. Martyne.

"Dandy!" agreed Tom.

"But we won't tell the girls until it's over," suggested Harry.

"Yes," spoke Buddy, "the G men told us to keep it secret. But we can make a report at a club meeting after it's all over."

"What a surprise it'll be!" chuckled Tom.

Buddy and his chums had all they could

do to keep the secret at the club meeting that evening. But Buddy held the proceedings to routine business. Reports of where more scrap could be obtained were turned in, committees were appointed to get it and a vote of thanks was given the girls for the new curtains.

Buddy and his chums told of their experience in the old factory.

"I—now—move that—now—this club does something to Sid Monson and his gang —now!" called Tommie Tasker.

"Second the motion—if not now as soon as possible," called out George Jackson.

There was a laugh and the motion was unanimously passed.

"How is our tin can drive coming along?" asked Buddy.

"I saw in the paper a piece that said Mountchester was behind other cities of its size in the county," said Frank Todd.

"Then we've got to get busy!" decided Buddy. "We've got to help Mountchester go over the top in the tin can drive. A lot of people still don't process their cans.''

"And a lot still put them in the ashes and garbage," added Tom.

"We'll start tomorrow," said Buddy "and put on a new drive."

This was generally agreed to and then the meeting adjourned.

It had been arranged that Buddy and his chums would go with Mr. Martyne, a little before midnight, to their observation post near the old stove factory.

"Now we must all keep very quiet," warned Buddy's father when he had let the auto coast to a secluded spot.

The waiting seemed very long in the darkness, illuminated only partially by a moon in its first quarter. Buddy and his chums sat silently in the auto. Now and again they thought they saw shadowy figures flitting to and fro around the old factory. But they could not be sure. Nor were they certain, if they did see men moving, whether they were the spies or the F.B.I. agents.

But, suddenly, from the interior of the

factory came a single shot. It was not muffled as it would have been had it been fired inside the ice box.

"I'm sure that was the G men's signal," whispered Buddy in Tom's ear.

"I hope it was," murmured Tom. "I'm stiff sitting still so long."

"Hark!" cautioned Harry.

Sounds of shouting voices came from within the old factory and then a rush of feet from the road beyond where Mr. Martyne had parked his car. Instantly the roadway was lighted brightly as several car search lights were turned on.

Buddy and his chums could see several men leaping out of the cars and running toward the old factory.

"They've got guns!" tensely whispered Tom.

"They're the G men," said Harry.

"Keep quiet!" cautioned Buddy.

"I think the need for silence has passed," said Mr. Martyne. "I believe this is the end.

The G men have rounded up the spies."

And so it proved. A little later, by the auto headlights and searchlights, Buddy and his chums saw a small group of prisoners being herded out of the factory by the G men and into cars in waiting. A number of autos were ranged up and down the road in readiness.

A whistle was blown, another answered and several of the cars moved away in the darkness. A lone man approached the Martyne auto.

"Buddy's Victory Club?" asked a voice the boys recognized as that of Mr. Godfrey.

"Part of it," answered the club president.

"Well, you can do that heel-clicking trick again if you want to, Buddy," chuckled Mr. Godfrey.

"Did you get them all?" asked Mr. Martyne.

"Every last one of the gang. The raid was perfect. They were taken completely by surprise."

"Was anybody shot?" asked Buddy.

"No. That shot was only a signal for my men to close in. The gang of spies didn't have time to reach for any guns. They gave up without a struggle. I want to thank you boys again. And now I have some information for you."

"What?" asked Buddy.

"It's about those sash weights. I had one of my men investigate. That junkman in Prattville, Lou Farrish, has been buying them from a crowd of boys. Sid Monson was one. And we found some weights with red paint on. Yours, I imagine, Mr. Martyne."

"Very likely," assented Buddy's father.

"What happened to 'em?" asked Buddy.

"The junkman agreed to turn them in, with a lot of other iron junk he had unlawfully bought from Sid Monson. It will all go into the Mountchester scrap quota. And there are a lot of tin cans, too, that Sid and his crowd admitted taking away illegally from Mountchester dumps."

"Oh, then you talked with Sid?" asked Tom.

"Our men talked with him and *to* him," chuckled Mr. Godfrey. "I don't believe he'll give you boys any further trouble."

"Did he lock us in that ice box?" asked Buddy.

"Yes, he and his cronies. He said he didn't realize how dangerous it was. And Sid said he planned to come back later and raise the bar. He did, he says, but found you had already gotten out. If you want to have him arrested——"

"No," said Mr. Martyne, "I think we'd better let the matter drop. They won't do it again, very likely."

"Not if they know what's good for them," said Mr. Godfrey significantly. "Well, it's all over now. I must hurry to see about locking up the spies. They'll be tried later and I think sent away for long terms. Our evidence is conclusive. Good night!"

"Good night," echoed Buddy and his chums.

"It wasn't such a spectacular raid as I thought it would be," Tom complained as they drove back to Mountchester.

"The F.B.I. doesn't believe in fireworks," said Mr. Martyne. "The G men do their work quietly but efficiently."

"I'll say they do!" remarked Buddy.

The Victory Club was quite excited at the next meeting listening to the stories told by Buddy and his chums. They could not hear enough and planned to visit the old stove factory and ice box prison.

"Will the dictaphone be there yet?" asked Agnes.

"And can we talk over it?" inquired Lucy Gordon.

"I don't know," said Buddy. "I think the G men probably took it away."

Such proved to be the case. But Buddy's girl and boy friends got quite a thrill merely by going in the ice box. They looked at the attempts the boys had made to cut a hole through the door.

Some inquiries Buddy made a little later, of old residents in the neighborhood of the stove factory, disclosed that the "secret room" was, really, an old ice box. The factory had, at one time, been a country hotel and food had been kept in the big, almost air-tight store room.

The boys also learned that the heavy boxes they had noticed in the shack held the dictaphone apparatus installed by the F.B.I. agents.

Buddy and his chums made another inspection of the old ice box.

"We would have had to whittle a week to cut a hole," observed Tom as he noted the thickness of the portal.

"Yes, it's a good thing the girls rescued us," said Buddy.

"What say we give 'em a party? I mean couldn't the Club give the girls a party?" asked Tom.

"Sure!" said Harry.

"Sure!" agreed Buddy, and in token he

clicked his heels three times. "But first," he added, "we've got to get in more scrap and tin cans."

To such good end did the members of the Victory Club work in the next week, that when the monthly report was printed in the paper, Mountchester had gone over the top!

"Not only in iron and rubber," said Mr. Martyne as he read it to his wife, "but in tin cans. And listen to this:

" 'No small praise for the success of the tin can drive must be given the Victory Club of which Richard (Buddy) Martyne is president.'

"Doesn't that make you feel proud of Buddy, Mother?"

"Yes, it does," said Mrs. Martyne with a happy smile.

The salvage drive in Mountchester did not end with this. There was more iron, rubber and tin to gather to help toward victory. But there were no more spy or saboteur activities in that area for a long time.

The men arrested by the F.B.I. received long prison terms.

Sid Monson and his crowd kept well out of the way of Buddy and his chums.

"They know when they're licked," said Tom.

"If they don't we can show 'em," boasted Harry.

"Oh, let 'em alone," advised Buddy. "We have other things to do."

"Such as what?" asked Harry.

"Getting up that party for the girls who got us out of cold storage," chuckled the red-haired boy. "The club is going to throw a party for not only the girls, but everybody."

"Who's giving the party?" asked Tom.

"I am," said Buddy with a wink. "But dad's paying for it," he added and joined with his chums in the laughter that followed.

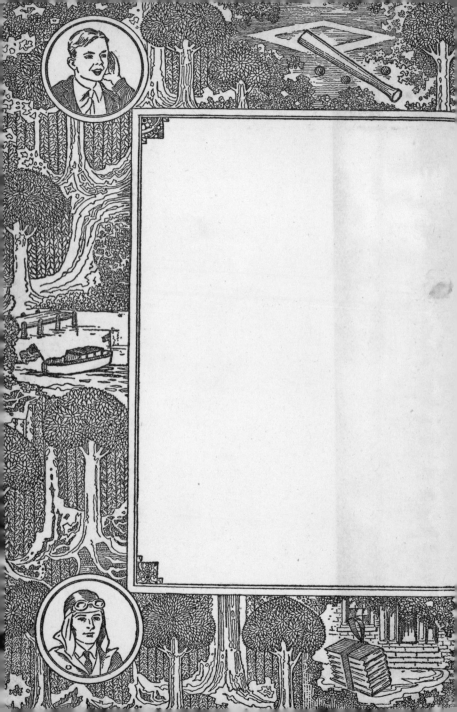